Station Bound

Prequel for the Artemis series

David Miller

Firmament Books

Before the Moon, there was the Station—and the man who had to leave everything behind to reach it.

For rookie Canadian astronaut George Scorby, the road to the International Space Station is paved with endless hours in the Neutral Buoyancy Lab and the cold, technical mastery of the Canadarm2. In 2018, as the world looks toward the promise of the Artemis program, George finds himself "Station Bound"—assigned to a six-month rotation in low Earth orbit that secures his career but may cost him a seat on the first missions back to the Moon.

Station Bound is a visceral Hard SF novella that captures the high-stakes journey of a modern astronaut. From the grueling underwater simulations in Houston to the isolated quarantine of the Baikonur Cosmodrome, George must balance the rigorous demands of the Soyuz launch sequence with the quiet, domestic sacrifices of a man leaving his world behind. As a man of deep conviction, he navigates his roles as husband, father, and astronaut, knowing that once the engines ignite, there is no turning back.

This foundational prequel to the *Artemis* series offers an authentic, behind-the-scenes look at the twilight of the ISS era. It is a story of technical precision, personal sacrifice, and the unwavering discipline required to lead humanity toward a new lunar future. The engines are lit. The journey begins.

First published 2026 by David Miller in Australia

Published by Firmament Books.

ISBN 978-0-6457134-3-5 (Ebook), 978-0-6457134-4-2 (Paperback)

Cover Design: Book Cover Design by Miltart.

firmamentbooks.com

davidmiller.online

"The more you know, the less you fear. We spend years preparing for every possible contingency so that when the unexpected happens, it's just another problem to solve." — **Chris Hadfield, Canadian Astronaut.**

"When I look out the window and see the Earth, all the elements are what you would expect from the design of a creative God. It just strengthens my faith. I wish there were words to describe what it's like." — **Jeffrey Williams, NASA Astronaut.**

Contents

1

Wednesday 14 March 2018

George Scorby released the rail he was gripping with his right hand on the outside of the International Space Station (ISS) and reached for the roll of cable tethered nearby. Transferring it to his left hand, he floated free from the station. A short strap tethered him so he couldn't float far, and another retractable safety line attached to the back of his waist. He carefully freed the end of the cable and plugged it into a socket in front of him.

"Okay, CONTROL, I've plugged cable J743 into socket CA1B," said George. "Dave, you can screw the connector on now."

George moved slightly to his left, and Dave floated over and placed the pistol grip tool (PGT), an electric screwdriver, in place to drive the screw on the connector home. Air bubbles and a diver came into his view and replaced the fake PGT that Dave had been holding with a working PGT, which Dave then used to secure the connector.

They were in the Neutral Buoyancy Lab at NASA's Johnson Space Center in Houston, a massive 12-metre deep pool of crystal-clear water. Preparations were underway for George's initial spacewalk. They were installing a redundant power cabling system for the multi-jointed robotic Canadarm2 on the ISS. As a Canadian astronaut, he was the mission specialist for Canadarm2.

Dave, a veteran of two shuttle missions to the ISS and two previous spacewalks, was the experienced member of the team. He received the 'fake' drill, which was neutrally buoyant, back from the diver and gave George the go-ahead to run the cable.

George unrolled a couple of metres of the relatively stiff cable. Every metre or so along the cable were clips that enabled it to be secured to the station. He located the first one and secured it in the cable tray running along the outside of the station. Then he eased another metre to his left, sliding his tether along the handrail, unrolling the cable a bit and securing the following clip in the cable tray. The cable was ten metres long, so he repeated this action another eight times, needing two careful reconnections of his tether to the rail at junctions. It was a slow, laborious process, exacerbated by his body occasionally floating into an unhelpful orientation. Very tiring.

Finally, he could plug in the other end of the cable. On his radio, he said, "Control, I've plugged the other end of J743 into socket CA1A. Time for Dave's work."

"Copy that, George."

Dave secured the cable, and then they floated back and surveyed their work.

"Gentlemen," said the mission controller, "that is all we have on the list of work. So, we will transition you out of the tank. Your divers will take you over to the crane."

Both Dave and George copied the information.

George relaxed. It would take a while for them to return to the surface as they needed to allow the nitrogen to come out of their bloodstreams since they had been at the bottom of the pool for almost six hours.

In another month, he would fly to Moscow, to Space City, to complete last-minute training there on the Soyuz capsule he would fly in to the ISS. Both SpaceX and Boeing were developing craft for NASA's Commercial

Crew Program, which would give NASA its own access to the ISS for the first time since the end of the Shuttle program. However, neither had yet had its first crewed flight. So, he would spend a month in Moscow before his family joined him to travel to the Baikonur Cosmodrome in Kazakhstan. At least it would be summer, and he wouldn't have to endure a Russian winter!

He stretched his muscles while he waited on the crane platform. Dave was behind him, facing the opposite direction. He felt the platform slowly rise several metres, and he equalised the pressure in his sinuses.

"George, let's go to channel two for a chat," said Dave on the radio.

"Copy that, switching to channel two," said George. This would give them a degree of privacy, but CONTROL could still reach them if needed.

"That went well," said Dave.

"Yeah, we seemed to keep to the timeline pretty well this time. I'm not sure how I'm going to be letting go like that in space."

"Just take it slow and breathe, test and double-check. It'll be freaky the first time you do it! Have you heard anything about Artemis?"

There were rumours that the NASA Astronaut Office would select the astronauts for the Artemis program soon.

"No," said George, "have you?"

"Na, but I thought you might have since they are looking to put a Canadarm2 on the Lunar Gateway station."

"I know they are talking with the CSA, but I haven't heard anything definite."

"I hear that if they sign, they are going to get an astronaut on Artemis 2," said Dave. "That would almost definitely mean you get to orbit the moon."

"I don't know. There are two others in training, and this mission probably rules that out."

"What! They'd send a newbie on a moon mission! Na, you are a shoo-in."

"What are you up to this weekend, Dave?"

"Nothing in particular. The kid's with my ex, so I might go out with some mates. You?"

George took a sip of his drink using the drinking straw in his helmet. Again they moved shallower.

"We are taking the boat out for a sail. There are not many weekends before we ship off to Moscow, so it's time to make some memories."

"Good idea. In our job, you always have to be prepared for the unexpected. Make good memories with them."

2

LATER THAT DAY

Arriving home in his SUV, George pulled into the garage. He felt tired. He grabbed his briefcase and headed into the house by the internal door. Nate, their youngest son, was helping Jean prepare dinner.

"Hi, honey. Something smells good," said George, giving her a hug and kiss. "Howdy, Nate."

"Hi, George, this will be ready soon," said Jean.

"Dad! I came first in our math quiz today!" said Nate excitedly.

"Wow, that's great!" said George, rubbing Nate's head. "Where's your brother?"

"He's upstairs studying."

"Why don't you go upstairs and tell him we are ready for dinner."

"Sure, Dad," said Nate, running off.

"It's not quite ready yet," said Jean.

"That's okay. Family time doesn't hurt," said George. "How's your day been?"

"Not too bad. Only three classes today, and they were the good ones. How about you?"

"All day in the Neutral Buoyancy Lab, so I'm pretty tired. I was thinking of taking Kevin to the dock after dinner, restocking the boat, and doing some maintenance. Is that okay?"

"Fine with me."

"Hi, Dad," said Kevin as he and Nate came down the stairs.

"How are you, Kev?" asked George, giving him a hug.

"Good."

"How about you and I go down to the boat after dinner, and we can prep it for the weekend?"

"Um, OK."

"Great. I'm really looking forward to this weekend. The weather looks great."

"Can I come too?" asked Nate.

"Not tonight," said George. He really wanted to spend some time with Kevin alone. He was growing up quickly.

"Boys, do you want to set the table?" said Jean.

After dinner, Kevin, and George stopped at a pharmacy for drinks and snacks on their way to the dock where their yacht.

George parked the car, and he and Kevin hopped out. They walked to the back of the car, opened the trunk, and picked up their bags of snacks.

They walked together out onto the dock in the cooler evening air, the boats gently lapping against their moorings.

"Beautiful night," said George.

Kevin grunted.

They clambered onto their boat.

"Can you check the engine oil and fuel while I put this stuff in the galley," said George.

"Yup," said Kevin.

Yep, teenage boys don't say much, thought George.

"How's school?"

"Ok."

"Your classes going ok?"

"Yep."

"Need any help with anything?"

"Nope."

Open questions, thought George. Must ask open questions.

"What sport are you thinking of playing in the summer?"

"Probably football."

"Who else is playing?"

"Maybe Frank and James."

"Great! Okay, let's check the sails. I'm not sure we got the spinnaker bagged properly last time. Can you find the bag?" If they hadn't, it would be a bit of work.

Kevin dove into the bow of the yacht and located the bag, pulling it out. "The two cleats are properly in place," he said, and after opening the top of the bag, "And the head is on top and it looks properly packed. Were you worried it was twisted?"

"Maybe. It was brought down in a hurry. Maybe your mum packed it."

"I think it will be okay."

"Okay, the worst that will happen is a twist, and it's not like we will be racing. You know, if this were something at work, we would repack it to be sure."

"That must be a pain."

"Yes, but we want to be safe, so it's worth it. What do you think about my trip to spend 6 months on the ISS?"

"I think it's cool!"

"I'm cool now! Let's go check the rigging, eh?" said George, leaving the cabin and heading on deck. "Are you worried that something might go wrong?"

"No, not really," said Kevin, following George onto the deck. "Nothing ever goes wrong."

"Hmm, well, that's not true. Things go wrong all the time; we just manage it well and have backups if it's important."

"So, nothing really goes wrong."

"Most of the time. But it is still dangerous. It's a bit like sailing. We can check this rigging, but we won't see that there is a weakness up towards the top of the mast where we can't see. Then we hit a strong wind and a stay breaks and the mast snaps and smashes down on deck."

"But that's never happened to us, and we get the rigging checked every season," said Kevin.

"Yes, we do. But will that stop it from happening?"

"It might if they discover the problem."

"But sometimes things go wrong even though someone checks them. Or we get caught in an unexpected storm with too much sail up, and the stresses are too high for the rigging."

"Okay, that could happen, I guess."

"Well, even though we've done all we can to reduce risks and prepare, things can still go wrong during my flight, and you need to be prepared for that."

"So, you could get hurt?"

"Yep, or worse. Do you remember that astronauts died on two shuttle missions?"

"But you aren't flying on the shuttle. They shut it down because it was dangerous."

"Yes, that was part of the reason, and I'm flying on the Soyuz, which has been very safe. Even so, things can still go wrong."

"But God will keep you safe."

"God will keep me safe in a spiritual sense, and I'll never be separated from him, but he doesn't promise that I won't die."

"But we'll be praying for you, and he has to answer our prayers."

"He will definitely hear your prayers, but he may not answer them in the way you want. Do you think Jesus wanted to die?"

"He died because he loves us," said Kevin.

"That's not what I asked. Did he want to die?"

"I don't know."

"What did Jesus pray for in the Garden of Gethsemane?"

"Ahh, for his friends."

"Yes, he did, and what else?" said George, handing Kevin a halyard to rewind.

"Hmm, to take the cup of poison from him."

"Yes, and not his will but God's be done?"

"Oh, yeah."

"So he didn't want to die, and asked God to take it away, but he submitted to his Father's will. What does that tell you?"

"That God does what he wants."

"I guess so, saying it crudely. It was God's will for Jesus to die for us, because of His love for us. If it is God's purpose for me to die on this mission, then prayer isn't going to change that."

"Then why pray at all?"

"Because many things are changeable through prayer. How can I explain? When we are watching Doctor Who, can the Doctor change everything?"

Kevin looked thoughtful. "He wants to, but it seems he can't. There are fixed points in time that can't be changed."

"But he can change other things, but usually with consequences. Except that God is real and can change all things. God could have saved Jesus from death, but then Jesus would not have saved us. Does that make sense?"

"Sort of. Is this mission dangerous?"

"All space missions are dangerous to some extent," said George, "but we manage the risks. I've got a couple of spacewalks, but they aren't particularly dangerous. Not like the Moon missions will be.

"I think we've done all we need to do here. Let's pack everything up so we can head home."

Kevin stood in front of him. “Dad, I want you to come home.”

“I know, son. I do too. But if something happens, I want you to know God will look after you. And look after your mum and Nate.”

Kevin wrapped his arms around him, and George hugged him back.

They secured the yacht and walked back to the car.

3

MONDAY APRIL 9 2018 – HOUSTON

George and Dave, his Mission commander, sat drinking coffee in the cafe at the entrance of building 11 of the NASA Johnson Space Center. They both had meetings later in the morning with the Chief Astronaut about future flight prospects, and specifically the Artemis 2 mission, which would be the first manned deep space mission since Apollo.

"How was your week away?" asked Dave.

"It was great to be away from here, see family, and celebrate Easter with our church and family in Toronto," said George. "The kids loved it."

"That's right, you Christians had your death celebrations. And don't you Canadians even have public holidays for it? A travesty, lacking the separation of church and state."

"Umm, yes, we remember Jesus's death for us and his resurrection on the Sunday. I think you'll find Canada isn't the only country to have public holidays at Easter. Australia does too."

"Yep, socialists all of them."

"But socialists don't support Christianity, Dave."

"Then they're confused socialists holding on to old traditions. I bet most people in those countries don't even go to church."

"Probably true. We had a good time anyway. It was good to have some family time before we leave for Russia. You took time off, didn't you?"

"Yeah, my wife let me take the kid down to Florida. We did a couple of parks, which was fun. Goofy freaks me out still, though. And he just jumps out in front of you," Dave said.

"I'd of thought a decorated Air Force pilot, and NASA astronaut could cope with a cartoon dog."

"I get chills just thinking about it."

"I think we'd better make sure there's no Goofy on the ISS."

"Oh, that's put me in a spin. Goofy on the ISS. Thanks, man, now I'll have nightmares about that."

George laughed. He made a mental note to order a Goofy doll to take in his kit to the ISS.

"Did Juliet have a good time, even if you were running around hiding from Goofy?"

"She loved it. And we went and saw Shamu, sat right down the front and got wet. Great fun. You know they are stopping the Orca shows? Damn shame."

"No, I didn't."

"Yeah, political correctness gone mad, after some trainer died, and there was some movie. But the shows are full all the time."

"What are you hoping for from your meeting with Roger?" asked George. Roger Glen was the Chief Astronaut.

"Maybe an Artemis assignment, but I think they are putting the young ones on that mission. And I'm not different enough to qualify. More likely another ISS mission, or maybe a ride testing one of the new commercial crew systems, but I think they are taken," said Dave.

"I hope I can get that Artemis 2 seat. At least there are only four of us from the CSA who qualify."

"Yeah, you've got a better chance than I do. But do you really want the mission that doesn't land?"

"There'll be other missions later. I can't see them putting a Canadian on Artemis 3 for the landing."

"Maybe, if the program doesn't get cancelled. Mind you, I guess it's a guaranteed seat, so don't turn it down if it's offered."

George looked at his watch. "I guess we better head up, your meeting is in five minutes." He stood up, pushing back his chair, disposing of his cup in the trash, and they walked to the foyer.

Half an hour later, George was sitting in the waiting area outside Roger Glen's office watching Trish, his secretary, work at her computer, typing up something. The office door opened and Dave walked out.

"I think that'll be a good plan, Dave," said Roger. "We'll firm everything up once you return from the ISS."

"Thanks, Roger," said Dave, shaking Roger's hand.

"George, come on in," said Roger as George stood up. "How are you feeling about your ISS mission?"

"Great," said George as they walked into Roger's office and took their seats around his modest desk. "Everything is going to plan, and we'll be flying to Moscow soon."

"And you are getting on with Dave?"

"Yeah. He's a great guy and knows his stuff. He can be a bit rough around the edges, but we get on ok."

"That's good. I wanted to talk to you both before you left about future missions, especially since we are starting to work out crew roster for the Artemis Lunar missions."

"Yes, that and the commercial crew program look exciting."

"I've been talking to your bosses at CSA. They have decided that you will not be on Artemis 2 prime crew. There's a possibility that you might be on the backup crew since there are so few active Canadian astronauts. I'm sorry, but that is probably disappointing."

George slumped in his chair. "I'll be honest, it is disappointing. I thought I had a good chance at that mission."

"And you did, however CSA have decided to fly one of their more experienced crew. I can't confirm which one to you at this time. I think, given your background, that they would like to see you part of a crew that lands, and goes to the Gateway."

"I suppose that is of some consolation, however the fourth mission probably isn't going to be until 2025 or 2026 at the earliest."

"That's true, and you wouldn't be the first astronaut to have a long period between missions. We hope that, once the commercial crew program flights are underway, that all western astronauts may have more opportunities than there have been in recent years."

"Sir, are there any CSA seats scheduled in future Artemis missions?"

Roger said, "We haven't made any decisions on that matter yet, but I expect someone with your credentials will participate in flights that include the Gateway for the Canadarm2 commissioning."

"Hmm. As I said, it's disappointing."

"I suggest you focus on your upcoming mission. There's lots of good work you'll be doing there. This is your first flight, and you've had to wait a while for it. Once you're back home and fit, we will talk again and see what opportunities there are for you."

"Yes, I am looking forward to this flight after all this time, so I will try to focus on it."

"Great. All the best for your mission in case we don't see each other before you leave," said Roger, standing up and showing George out.

"Thankyou, sir. All the best to your wife."

"Yes, same to Jean. Margaret was planning to meet up with her while you are in Moscow."

"That would be good. Thank you.

George left the office and returned to his desk to ponder his future.

As George logged into his computer to check his email, Dave walked over to him.

"Did you get it?" asked Dave.

"No, they think it would be better for me to be on a mission that lands and goes to the Gateway. Maybe I'll commission the CanadaArm2 there."

"Bummer. I just got a commercial crew flight spot."

"That's great news, Dave! Congratulations!"

"Yeah, I'm excited. It's the first non-test SpaceX flight to the space station next year."

"That's fantastic. I hope the rest of the crew is good to work with."

"I'll let you know how it goes. In the meantime, let's focus on our upcoming mission."

"Agreed. I'm looking forward to it."

As the two astronauts returned to preparing for their mission, George couldn't help but feel a mix of disappointment and excitement about what the future might hold. He knew he had to make the most of his ISS mission and continue to work hard to increase his chances of being on future missions. The universe was vast, and there was still so much to explore and discover. And he was determined to be a part of it all.

4

SATURDAY APRIL 14 2018

George, Jean, Nate, and Kevin were awake early and at the dock in Clear Lake, where their yacht True North was moored, ready to sail for the day. The day was bright and clear, and the waters of the lake sparkled in the sunlight. A light breeze rippled the surface of the lake,gently cooling George's skin in the warm sun.

"Okay, Nate," said George. "Can you help your mum stow our gear, please, while Kevin and I hoist the sails?"

"Aww, I wanted to do that," said Nate.

"Don't worry, I'm sure we'll still have plenty left to do if we put this stuff away quickly," Jean said.

"Okay," said Nate, reluctantly picking up a bag from the dock. Jean joined him, and they started stowing their lunch items and spare clothes.

George and Kevin headed into the bow of the yacht, opening the hatch and hauling the sail bags up and out onto the deck.

"Okay, Kev," said George, "we'll start with the mainsail as usual. Do you want to start unzipping the boom bag? I'll uncleat the halyard."

"Sure, Dad," said Kevin. "It looks like we'll have a bit of wind today, which will be fun."

"It sure will be. I'm sorry we couldn't invite your friends today, but I wanted some time with just us as a family."

"That's okay. I understand now that you've explained it."

George was amazed. Two days earlier they had had a full-on fight when he had said Kevin's friends could not come out on the sail. Parenting a teenager was not easy. Jean would have her work cut out for her while he was away.

It took them about twenty minutes to prepare all their sails and stow their gear. Once they were ready, George started the motor, and Jean steered the vessel out of the docks and down Clear Creek, under the road bridge and into the waters of Trinity Bay.

George, Kevin, and Nate raised and set the mainsail and jib as a well-practiced team.

The yacht glided smoothly through the waters of Trinity Bay and the four of them were soon away from the high-density buildings of Houston buildings. The horizon was filled with beach houses and farmland, and the only sound was the gentle sloshing of the waves against the hull of the boat and the wind whistling through the rigging.

They spent the morning catching up and chatting as they sailed down the bay. As they went, they marvelled at the presence of the sea life that surrounded them. Dolphins leapt from the waves, and fish of all shapes and sizes skirted underneath the surface of the water.

Brown pelicans followed the boat as they sailed back to Smith Point which separated Trinity and Galveston Bays.

Soon, they arrived at Galveston Bay, and the sights and sounds of the bay filled their senses. The water was much different here than it had been in Trinity Bay. Here, the sea was filled with a variety of marine life; seagulls, jellyfish, and even an occasional shark were all visible.

As they sailed into Galveston Bay, they discussed their plans for the future. George was preparing to fly to Moscow to begin training for his upcoming mission on the Soyuz spacecraft to the International Space Station.

His family were eager to hear more about his mission and all the excitement that was to come.

Sailing to a point, they anchored the boat. The boys jumped into the water for a swim, while Jean and George laid out lunch.

Nate and Kevin sat across from George over lunch, peppering him with questions about his mission.

"What do you think you'll see out there?" Nate asked.

"Oh, I'm sure it will be amazing," George replied with a smile. "The stars will be points of light that don't twinkle. I'll be able to see so much of the earth."

Kevin leaned forward in his chair. "Do you think you're ready, whatever might happen?"

George nodded, his enthusiasm evident in the sparkle of his eyes. "I've never been to space before, so of course I'm excited, but I'm also nervous. But the team and I have been training for a long time for this."

"And what is your main job there?" asked Kevin.

"I'm a Mission Specialist. So my main focus is the Canadarm2 and maintaining and running different experiments. I have a spacewalk too."

"So you get to fly around in space alone, cool," said Nate.

"No, dummy. He's attached to the ISS," said Kevin.

"It's not a dumb question. I'll be with Dave, my commander, and we'll both be attached to the ISS, so no free floating," said George.

"It still sounds fun," said Nate.

"It will be," said George, "but there will be all the day-to-day stuff of cleaning up stuff, just like we do at home."

"So you don't have robots to do that?" asked Nate.

"To clean up? No. We are still trying to design suitable robots. There's one we are trialling that looks like the upper half of a man, we call Robonaut, and a really new one called Astrobee, which is a cube that uses fans to move around."

"Cool. I like robots."

George laughed, "Yes, I know!" The Scorby household regularly requested WALL-E and Robots for movie night.

After they had finished their lunch, Jean said, "Let's pray for your Dad.

"Father, thank you for the great man that You've given me as a husband, and as a father to Kevin and Nate. Thankyou that he loves Jesus and seeks to serve Him. As he goes on this great adventure into space, I pray that You will keep him safe, keep him honouring You and showing Your love to those he is with. Help him to resist sin. Help him to see Your glory in all he sees, as we see Your glory now in this beautiful bay. Help him remember that we love him, and You love him more than he can ever know. In Jesus' name we pray this."

And they all said, "Amen."

George was teary and hugged Jean and the boys. "That was beautiful, thank you," he said, giving her a kiss.

As the day went on, so did the beauty around them. Galveston Bay was full of life, and it was an ever-changing tapestry of color, life, and adventure. The wind increased, and they took the opportunity to practice their tacking and jibing, enjoying working as a team.

At dusk, the yacht pulled back into the waters of Clear Creek, and the satisfactorily tired family of four tidied up the True North and docked. It wasn't long before they all piled into their SUV and George drove them the short drive home, picking up some chicken from Chick-fil-A on the way.

George was glad it had been a great family day. It would not be long before he left them to fly to Moscow. He hoped there would be more days like this with them in the future.

5

TUESDAY 24 APRIL 2018

George and Dave sat in the back of the bouncing van as they were driven through the early morning Moscow traffic from Sheremetyevo International Airport to Star City. There they would undertake their final training and reviews prior to the launch to the ISS in a Soyuz capsule.

It had been a long flight. First, there was the two-and-a-half-hour flight from Houston to O'Hare, Chicago, and then the 14-hour flight to Moscow, after a two - hour layover to complete International check-in. They had had dinner at a bar at O'Hare, enjoying their last taste of American food for several months.

George looked out of the window at the grey landscape on the cool spring day. Occasionally he saw flashes of colour, but most of the view from the car was of grey buildings. Freeways rarely presented a fair representation of a city, and that was true for Moscow. He could see none of the colourful, red iconic Moscow buildings and churches.

The scenery changed to forest as they skirted around the northeast of the city as they headed to the formerly top-secret cosmonaut training base.

Finally, the van turned off the freeway, travelling on some minor roads to the enclave hidden in the forest.

Zvezdnyi Gorodok today looks nothing like it did forty years ago. George saw modern apartment buildings, hotels, and recreation facilities and only the occasional old concrete structures of the original base, though the name Star City remains. They drove past a modern hotel with a busload of Russian tourists eager to soak up the space-related culture of Russia's most famous cosmonaut training facility. Not unlike his experience at NASA facilities.

The van stopped outside the "Prophylactory", a three-floor dormitory built during the Apollo-Soyuz project that would be George and Dave's home for the next few weeks. It seems the designer was blind, judging by the top-floor windows and dark brown dormitory walls. The distinct Soviet styling of the metalwork window frames and sliding windows was an architectural period that looks to have ended in the 1970s.

As they stepped out of the van onto the pavement, the crisp spring air filled their lungs with a freshness that they had not experienced in a long time. The smell of pine trees permeated the air with a hint of something else, something that George could not identify.

Jean had warned him about the loneliness and the monotony of living in the cramped quarters of the ISS for three months, but George was looking forward to it. He would have time to read and reflect, do some writing, and work on his plans to be part of the upcoming lunar missions.

As they settled into their rooms at the 'Prophy', George felt energised. Perhaps it was the anticipation of floating weightlessly in space or the knowledge that he was about to embark on a mission that would take him to a place only a few have experienced.

George and Dave had travelled to Star City multiple times, spending countless hours studying the intricacies of the Soyuz spacecraft and Roscosmos systems. They had honed their Russian language skills to a point where they were fluent. The Russian space agency had given them clearance for flight in their vehicle, which was now the only way for NASA to launch astronauts to the ISS after the end of the US Shuttle flights. While the Commercial Crew program promised a human-rated launch capability for NASA, it had yet to deliver on that promise.

After unpacking and cleaning up, the astronauts met in their common room and made some coffee as they waited for the third team member for their mission, cosmonaut Yuri Malenchenko, to arrive.

“Ahh, there’s nothing like Russian instant coffee,” said Dave. The coffee was strong and sweet. “I’m glad they’ve discovered proper espresso style again, not this instant crap.”

George laughed. “I am looking forward to some of Yuri’s wife’s home cooking.”

Dave nodded in agreement. “I am too. I heard she is an amazing cook.”

“Ah yes, Russian cuisine is definitely one of a kind!” said George with enthusiasm.

“Indeed,” echoed Dave. “Makes me nostalgic just thinking about all the borscht and pelmeni I used to have over here! And don’t even get me started on their pirogi, blini, and the solyanka soups. It’s like they can turn anything into a great meal - no matter how humble it looks!”

George chuckled. “I’m looking forward to an olivier salad and shashlik khorovod! Grilling meat chunks wrapped in thin bread dough. Simply brilliant!”

“You’ll eat some of my shashlik this weekend then,” said Yuri, a short, fit, stocky man with dark hair. He walked over and gave each of them a mighty hug. “It’s great to see you guys.”

“Yuri, it’s good to see you,” said Dave. “I hope your family are well.”

“Yes, they are ruining my life. I hope you were able to bring those gifts I asked for?” asked Yuri in his heavily accented English.

“Yes,” said George. “Jean went and selected them herself. But you know we only have boys, so hopefully, she got the clothes that Russian teen girls are looking for!”

"That's great. We better start speaking Russian so we can help get you thinking Russian again. I'll take you over to the briefing now."

Yuri lead George and Dave into the briefing room. Seated at the basic, yet functional table, were Nikolai Konstantinov, Chief Engineer; Sergei Petro, Mission Director; and Yelena Petrovna, Medical Director. They greeted each other, all having met previously. Dave and George's fluency in Russian meant they would mostly conduct the briefing in Russian, clarifying in English when necessary.

The briefing was straightforward. For the next three weeks the crew would undertake medical tests and final revision training on the Soyuz and Russian ISS segment. Then their families would join them, and they would fly to the Baikonur Cosmodrome in Kazakhstan for the launch. They had a series of launch windows over 3 days.

Traditionally, both the Space Shuttle and the Soyuz and Progress spacecraft had taken two days, or 34 orbits, to rendezvous with the ISS. Roscosmos, the Russian Space Agency, had developed a fast, two-orbit rendezvous so that the crew could dock within three and a half hours after launch if all went well. If there were issues, they would revert to the longer approach. Their flight would be the first manned Soyuz flight to use the new approach method, so George and Dave needed to do some upgrade training on the new procedures and flight software.

As the briefing closed, George reviewed his schedule for the next three weeks. It was full and left little downtime. He had convinced Sergei to free up Sundays so that they at least had one day of rest. The additional flight training had compressed their schedules significantly.

"Yuri, I assume that you have already completed training on these new procedures?"

“Yes, of course,” Yuri replied.

“Do you think we need all this extra training?” George asked.

“Yes, at least Dave does. You just get to read your book during the launch!”

“I reckon we should have come a week earlier,” said Dave.

Soon, the backup crew would find out the same news during their briefing. They were deliberately isolated from the prime crew in case any of them got ill.

“Let’s go get changed,” said Dave. Their next activity would be a training session in the gym, combined with a medical Russian style.

An hour later they were all in the gym working up a sweat under the probing eyes of the mission medical team. Although George and Dave had already gone through a similar process with NASA, Roscosmos wanted them to pass their tests before letting them fly in the Soyuz.

George had been resting after his warm-up, and he walked over to the treadmill with an ECG machine sitting next to it. It was time for a stress test. The nurse administering it, Rina, asked him to remove his shirt and to sit down. She then attached the twelve leads of the ECG to his chest and abdomen. They were chilly as she stuck them to his skin. Once she was happy with the readings, she asked him to step onto the treadmill. Taking his blood pressure and she started the treadmill.

In the next fifteen minutes, George’s workload grew until he felt certain he would have a heart attack. And then it stopped, and he could sit down while the monitoring continued. He’d never liked stress tests, and the Russian ones were the worst. They seemed to go further than those run by NASA!

After he had cooled down, he underwent strength testing, then a reflex test, then a full body ultrasound, plus echocardiogram, a bone density scan, a full body CT, a lung capacity test, optical and audiometric tests, and to cap the day off, a 800 metre swim test, a 3 metre dive and a 25 metre underwater swim test.

It was brutal. During some of the medical tests, he could just lie there and rest, but nobody seemed to care that you'd just completed another 7 tests before this, including a 50 km bike ride!

Finally, the tests were complete, and George and Dave staggered back to their unit, where they both collapsed on their beds.

6

THURSDAY APRIL 26 2018, STAR CITY, RUSSIA

George clambered into the mock-Soyuz capsule. Yuri and Dave were already in the Commander and Pilot seats, so George wedged himself into his seat. Thankfully, they weren't wearing their spacesuits, which would have made it even hotter and cramped in the vehicle.

Today they were practising the new launch procedures. As mission specialist, his primary role was to watch and follow checklists at critical times. Almost all the work was performed by the others. But he needed to be here for some simulations so that he was familiar with the process, and so that he could 'be in the way' so that the others learnt how to work around him!

To while away the time, he had brought a tablet so he could catch up on some reading and emails, and listen to some music, activities he could also do during the long waits prior to the launch.

As Dave and Yuri started their checklist, George checked his email. There was one from Jean.

George,

I'm glad you survived your medical. Sounds brutal. I'm glad that Sofia liked the clothes I bought for her. Remember not to eat too much of her yummy food.

Nate and Kevin are well. Nate is moody as ever. I know he wants to be good, but he keeps answering back. I don't think I'm going to enjoy being a mum of a teen!

And then he goes and does something like suggest we all go to the ballpark, and he and Nate have a hit (see my photo) and we got some Chick-fil-A, and had a great time.

Make sure you find some time for a videochat. I'm looking forward to spending some time together.

We are praying for you.

Love, Jean.

The email brought a smile to George's face. He could taste the juicy, crispy chicken sandwich. Jean's closing reminded him that he hadn't had much time to himself to pray or read his Bible since he'd arrived in Russia. "Sorry, Lord," he prayed silently.

"George, we are ready for you now," said Dave, intruding on his thoughts.

"Right, what step are we up to?" asked George.

"Punkt tri punkt sem'," said Yuri.

George stared at him for a second and then opened his checklist to item 3.7. His role for the next twenty minutes would be to follow along, triple-checking the work, and during some complex operations, actually read out the items for the others to complete.

"Separation arm and cross-check," said George in Russian.

"Armed," said Yuri.

"Check," said Dave.

"Check," said George after checking the switch setting. "Confirm separation with control."

"Control, Soyuz, ready for separation," said Dave, keying his mic.

"Soyuz, go for separation," replied the controller.

Dave said, "confirmed go for separation."

"Press the separation initiation button," said George.

"Initiating separation," said Yuri, using his stick to press the separation button.

""Separation confirmed. Negative contact light," said Dave.

"Okay, I see what you mean. We are straight into antennae and solar panel deployment. Right, so next, arm radar antennae release, R4."

"Arm R4," said Yuri, switching R4 to armed.

"Check," said Dave.

"Check," said George, settling into his checklist role. They continued like this for the next hour. The simulated launch progressed smoothly. Little had changed in those procedures, but everything happened faster. Burns of the ship's thrusters happened much more frequently, and they only had two orbits of 90 minutes.

The simulation was mostly a nominal voyage, with only a couple of minor issues introduced by the trainers, and they stopped the simulation prior to docking.

George helped the others out of the capsule and then hauled himself out. They would have a brief lunch break and return for another round.

"How was that?" George asked Dave as they walked to the stolovaya, the canteen.

"Pretty intense," said Dave. "Once we reach orbit, everything happens very quickly. There's not a lot of downtime."

"Yeah, I noticed. But then we don't have to hang around in the Soyuz for 2 days."

"I don't know. I kind of like the slow road and living in each other's armpits." This wasn't Dave's first Soyuz flight. He'd travelled to the ISS in one, 4 years earlier.

As they entered the stolovaya, the aroma of borscht and kasha filled the air. George's stomach rumbled in response. He scanned the options and settled on beef stroganoff and mashed potatoes. He looked around.

Technicians, managers, and the odd cosmonaut, whom he recognized from previous trips, filled the room.

"Have you heard from your daughter, Juliet?" Yuri asked Dave.

"A little. You know teens. They're all focused on their lives. It's a busy year for her, and she's getting ready for finals."

"Is she coming to the launch?" George asked.

"I hope so. The tickets are booked, but she's worried about missing school."

"That's tough. Maybe she could just meet us at the launch site. That'd save a couple of days."

"Maybe, but it's the contingency dates that hurt if we scrub."

"My guys are itching to miss school and come to Russia. I'll pray she can come."

Dave snorted.

"Yes," said Yuri. "Important is family. I too pray she comes."

Dave scowled. "Oh, brother, are you guys going to have prayer meetings on the ISS? Keep me out of it."

They ate in silence for a while. George thought about his family back in Houston. They would be sleeping, waking up in a couple of hours. He missed sleeping with Jean. He missed the morning chaos of getting them all to school and work.

7

Saturday, May 12 2018

George paced nervously. Jean, Kevin, and Nate should be on their way from Sheremetyevo International Airport. He and the rest of the crew were now in isolation, so he couldn't meet them at the airport. He headed down to the shared lounge room in their building, wearing a mask to help protect him from any bacteria or viruses others may have.

As he entered the room, he heard a vehicle arrive outside, and car doors open and close. Moments later, Nate came running in.

"Daddy", he said, seeing George, ran to him and hugged him.

"Hi Nate, did you have a good flight?" said George.

Kevin entered next, with a bit more of the reserve of a teen. "Hi, Dad," he said.

"Kevin, hi."

And Jean walked in next. "George, it's so good to see you." Stopping when she saw the mask. "Can I kiss you?"

"Umm, we'll probably just have to hug for now," said George, giving her a hug. "How was the flight?"

"Oh, Dad, it was so fun. The Chicago airport is so big. Have you been there? We had to go underground to get to our plane!" said Nate.

"Yes, it is big. How about you, Kev?"

"It was long and boring. Can we go to bed somewhere?"

"Sure, you must be tired. Someone will drive you guys to your hotel, and you can clean up. We are all having a barbecue lunch with Yuri's family."

"Are you well?" asked Jean.

"Yes, I'm fine - oh, the mask. It's just part of the isolation protocols so we don't get sick on the station."

"And you've finished your training now?"

"We sure have. We'll all fly to Kazakhstan on Monday and launch on Wednesday, so we have to be ready!"

"And everything is looking good?" she asked with a questioning gaze.

"Yep, all is good."

"Ok, boys," said Jean. "Time to head to the hotel and a shower. We'll see your dad again at lunch, which isn't long."

Jean ushered the boys out, and George followed them outside, waving them off.

Dave and George arrived at Yuri and Anna's house before Jean and the boys.

"Welcome to my home, my friends," said Yuri, giving each of them a hug.

"Thank you for hosting us," said George.

"It is no problem. We eat outside so we are clean, yes? Juliet is coming, no?" asked Yuri.

"Not today," said Dave. "She arrives tomorrow afternoon."

"Ah, that is bad. She'll have to meet my Sasha in Baikonur."

Someone knocked on the door.

"That'll probably be Jean," said George, and he went with Yuri to greet the visitors.

Yuri opened the door, and indeed it was Jean, Kevin, and Nate. "Welcome Jean, to my house. You know George!"

"Uncle Yuri," cried Nate, running to the Russian and giving him a hug.

"Well, he hasn't forgotten you," said Jean.

"Come in, Kevin," said Yuri, giving Kevin a hug he couldn't avoid.

As they walked out into the yard, Yuri said, "Jean, boys, this is my wife, Anna, and my little fish, Sasha."

"Papa, you don't say little fish in English!" said Sasha, reddening.

"Welcome to our house. Jean, thank you so much for the gifts you sent," said Anna. "Ignore my daughter, she is just used to not having so many pretty American boys around."

George noticed Kevin admiring Sasha as she blushed.

In the yard, a square steel barbecue was smouldering on one side. Food covered a large table.

"Wow, this is a feast," said Jean.

"Our last meal," said Yuri. "After this we eat only packaged food and drink from bags. So we eat big, yes?!"

"We will definitely enjoy ourselves," said George.

"Yes, now, as good Russians, all the men will come to the barbecue, and all the women will talk food, or dresses, or whatever. Come."

George, Dave, Kevin, and Nate all dutifully followed Yuri, carrying a large tray of skewered meat.

"Nate, you help me put these on the barbecue. Careful, not too close, it is hot."

"Nate has really taken to Yuri, hasn't he?" said Dave to George.

"Yes. I think it's the Russian bear thing. He spent so much time with us training, and on our boat, that I think Nate sees him as an uncle!"

"Kevin," said Yuri. "You think my Sasha is pretty, yes?"

"Ahh," said a tongue-tied, red faced thirteen-year-old Kevin.

"She causes many boys to trip on their tongues. Just do not blow into your mustache."

Now Kevin was truly stumped.

"The boy definitely doesn't have a mustache, Yuri," said Dave.

"Hmm, maybe you should cool", said Yuri. "Don't puff through your mustache. It's a saying."

"Oh, you want him to play it cool," said George.

Just then, Sasha walked over. "Nate, my mother wants you to help with the drinks. Come with me."

"Oi, they move quick," exclaimed Yuri. "Be careful George, or we soon be brothers!"

George smiled. It was good to be with family, and his teammates felt like just that, family.

8

TUESDAY, 15 MAY 2018, BAIKONUR, KAZAKHSTAN

George lay next to Jean in his bed. The Russians were surprisingly lenient once the crew arrived in Baikonur. Jean rolled over and snuggled into his shoulder.

"I'm glad they let me stay," she said, stroking his chest. "I've missed being with you."

"I do too. It'll be six months until I return. Have you been managing okay with the boys?"

"So far, but they are at impressionable ages, especially Kevin."

"Were you able to get him to go to the church youth group?"

"Once. He's one of the youngest there, so feels a bit out of it."

"Hmm. Maybe try to meet up with the families of the other young ones so he gets to know them?"

"Yeah, that's an idea. I think Mandy and Phil's son is that age. I'll call them when I get back."

"And you've been able to cope with working and looking after the boys without me?"

"Yes. It's busy. I'm looking forward to the summer break, and I've got less hours next term, so it will be easier.

"Are you worried about tomorrow?" she asked.

"Not overly. The Russians are reliable and safe. And since we are paying them, they have the money to do things properly."

"So you are excited?"

"Yep. This is what I've been preparing for, for years. I'm still annoyed I didn't get a seat on Artemis 2, but going to the ISS is a dream. It'll be amazing to view God's creation from there."

"Yep, focus on what's here now, not what might be. Speaking about enjoying God's creation." Jean rolled on top of him and sat back on his thighs. "I think we need to enjoy some more before you have to go."

George smiled. Again.

9

WEDNESDAY, 16 MAY 2018, BAIKONUR, KAZAKHSTAN

George waved at his friends and family. Today, they separated once more. He'd spent time with them yesterday, having lunch together. This morning the crew had eaten a hearty Russian breakfast and then suited up. Their suits had been carefully pressure tested and now they were boarding the bus to take them to the Soyuz rocket.

Blowing a last kiss to Jean, he climbed on board with the others, together with a few technicians and managers.

The old bus started up and trundled to the launch stand, about half a kilometer away.

As they went around a corner out of view of the family and press, the bus pulled over.

"Time for a piss," said Yuri.

George looked at Dave in alarm.

"It's a Russian tradition since Yuri Gagarin. We pee on the bus's wheel."

"But we just got leak tested."

Dave shrugged and left the bus for his turn.

Leaving his seat, George carefully clambered out of the bus in time to see Dave complete his christening of the wheel.

"Your turn, George. It's good luck," said Yuri.

After completing the task and carefully zipping his suit back up, he took a moment to look around at the scene. It was a flat, desolate landscape, peppered with launch towers and radio dishes.

"Time to go," said Yuri as he climbed back onto the bus. Dave and George followed with the rest of the entourage.

That was another strange thing for George. There must be twenty people on the bus, not just technicians, but some Roscosmos managers as well.

A few minutes later they arrived at the launch pad, and two managers helped him from the vehicle and supported him while he walked to the gantry.

The Soyuz-2 rocket was massive, standing 46.3 metres high. The three-stage rocket had four liquid-fuel boosters strapped around its base like a fortress wall. Instead of having a tower gantry beside the rocket, the Russians used three large gantries that were hydraulically raised from the ground to wrap the rocket. Two of these would retract around 45 minutes before launch.

George felt his pulse rate increase and felt a tension in his stomach. He was about to go to space!

The managers wished them well, and the three of them climbed up onto the stairway on the gantry for a last photo.

They then turned and climbed the stairway up to the base of the elevator. When they arrived at the elevator, George was sweating profusely in the suit. The same thing had happened during training and practice. He couldn't wait to be connected to the cooling systems in the Soyuz.

The crew, plus three technicians, crammed into the small elevator, which took them up the rocket to the Soyuz capsule.

George took in the scene from the gantry while Dave entered the Orbital Module. Antenna and other launch sites were scattered around. Not exactly a pretty place. He wondered what Jean, and the boys were thinking. Hopefully, they weren't too worried. The Russians currently had an excellent safety record.

A few minutes later, it was his turn to enter the Orbital Module and drop through the hatch, and take the right-hand seat. Wearing the weighty spacesuit made the procedure awkward, but he had practiced it well. He slipped into his custom-fitted seat and connected his suit hoses and cables. He felt the cool air flowing. It was bliss. Next, he found his belts, latched and tightened them, and then reported his status on the communications channel.

Yuri dropped down from the Orbital Module and took his seat, and started belting himself in.

George found his checklists and made sure his pad was within reach and secured.

Once Yuri had secured himself, he said, "Okay guys, everyone cosy?"

"Yep, I'm ready, let's go," said Dave.

"I'm snuggled in, ready for my fast trip to the ISS. Are you going to deliver, Yuri?" said George.

"Sure. I'm feeling good, and I'm sure we'll have a quick ride. Okay, Dave, let's start this checklist."

It was almost two and half hours since they had entered the Soyuz capsule, and they were approaching T minus one minute. George's muscles were cramped in the chair, and he was looking forward to be able to leave his chair in around fifteen minutes. The pressure in his Sokol spacesuit made moving an effort. Below them, the Soyuz rocket was fueled and pressurised, and the last remaining umbilical masts were about to be retracted. They were sitting on top of a bomb, hoping to ride a controlled explosion that would thrust them into space. If something went wrong, the abort system would pull their capsule free from the rest of the rocket, putting them through up to merciless twenty-four-g.

George took a deep breath, mentally preparing himself for the upcoming launch. He thought back to all the training he had undergone, all the simulations he had run, and felt confident that he was prepared for anything that could go wrong.

He closed his eyes and began to silently pray, thanking God for the opportunity to witness His creation from a new perspective, and for the safety of himself and his crewmates.

"Here we go guys, T minus twenty. Engine ignition," said Yuri.

A massive vibration rippled through the rocket stack as the main core and four booster engines ignited. George could hear, or perhaps better said, feel the massive engines below them as they came up to full thrust fifteen seconds later.

He could feel the entire stack shaking and creaking as it fought against the tie-downs holding the rocket down until at T minus zero, they lifted off. There was not much that he could see out of the window near him. The initial acceleration was low but gradually increased. They expected a maximum of almost four-g just before the boosters separated at 1 minute 58 seconds.

Yuri and Dave were calling out milestones. Dave was able to reach his controls, but Yuri had to use a special stick to reach his controls, since he was in the centre seat and furthest from the displays.

The view outside the window darkened as they rode higher and faster. The acceleration pushed George further into his seat. It relaxed briefly as the engines throttled down for 'Max Q', maximum aerodynamic pressure, when the forces were greatest on the rocket. Unlike the others, George could just enjoy the ride. He followed along with the reports Yuri was making, but primarily he savoured the feelings and sound of the launch, and watched out the windows to see what he could. The sounds of the engines were diminishing as they rode higher into the atmosphere.

"Stage one separation," said Yuri.

The force from the engines dropped back to only a bit above normal gravity, and the boosters separated. The single engine (with four outlets) of core stage two was now driving them higher. They were already fifty kilometers high.

"That was quite a ride," said George.

"Yes, she is far gentler now," said Yuri.

Stage two had another three minutes to burn before stage two ignition. Rather than rapidly gaining altitude, they were now getting faster to reach the orbital velocity of the ISS. This meant that the rocket was closer to horizontal relative to the ground, and he could look out and see the Earth below him speeding by.

Before he knew it, Yuri was calling out, "Stage three ignition. Stage two separation."

The Soyuz 2 rocket featured a unique design called hot staging, where the Stage three engine ignited while Stage two remained attached. This required extra insulation to be added on top of the second stage, shielding it from the heat of the third stage startup and allowing for the third stage to not need ullage motors to push propellant and oxidizer to the engines.

The final stage would burn for four minutes, with the acceleration reaching three-g just before engine cutoff. During this burn, they had a planned 'wave at the cameras' event. Yuri would change the camera angles by prodding a switch with his stick, and they would each wave, showing the world that they were still alive. It was silly, but their families found it comforting, and their social media fans liked to see their favorite astronaut wave at the camera, so they all did their part.

Finally, around nine minutes after their launch, the third stage separated, and they were in zero-g.

After a minute, they could open their space suit visors and move around the cabin.

"Welcome to space, George," said Dave.

"Thanks, it's a real weight off my mind," said George.

Dave groaned.

George released his straps and floated up to the hatch that accessed the orbital module. After obtaining permission from mission control in Moscow, he unlatched the hatch and swung it open into the reentry capsule. That took up some space in the module, but they now had access to the orbital module's living area, which included a small toilet, a mini food preparation area. There was cargo stored in the living area, so it was a bit cramped.

George filled three drink bags with water and delivered two to his crewmates. Then he grabbed some snacks, returned to his seat and passed them around. With such a quick ride to the station, they would not bother removing their Sokol space suits.

Interception with the ISS had gone well. They had finished their approach, flying around the ISS, and were currently aligning to the docking port. The process was automated; however, Yuri and Dave could manually dock if required. The crew could see the docking alignments through a periscope in the front of the vehicle. However, everything was working perfectly, and the probe docked and locked the first time. In no time, latches secured the Soyuz to the ISS, and the hatches were opened. While the crew conducted pressure checks, the Soyuz crew changed out of their Sokol spacesuits into their blue flight suits, ready for the official photos.

After completing the leak checks and air sampling, they cracked open the hatch and swung it into the Soyuz's orbital module. Yuri, as commander, squeezed past the hatch first, pausing for the obligatory photo while chatting to the crew onboard taking the photos and operating the TV camera. Then Dave floated through for his photo and hugs, and finally George took his turn and joined the crowd in the small docking area.

They all knew each other. The current ISS crew comprised two Russians, Alexei Denisov as commander and Yevgeny Lazarev as a mission specialist, and one American, Steve Davidson, also a mission specialist.

After their initial greetings, they moved down to the Unity module, and prepared for the official ceremony where they would join the ISS Expedition 56 crew, and have the opportunity to talk briefly with friends and family at home, in this case, still at the launch site!

While they waited for the event to begin, he looked around the station. He'd already noticed the distinct smell of bodies and electronics. The module was clean and tidy, but showing a few signs of wear. It was amazing how familiar it seemed after many days of training in the mockup at the Johnson Space Centre.

The crew were energetically chatting in English and Russian while they set up the equipment and audio and video synchronised.

"ISS, we are ready to start the event," came the call from Mission Control.

The camera was fastened at the other end of the module. There were four headsets for the entire crew, and George, as the lone Canadian could wear one.

"Go ahead, Houston," said Alexei.

"Station, this is Julie Payette, Canadian Governor General and former astronaut, veteran of two space flights. How do you hear me?" came over the communication circuit. First in Russian, then in English.

Alexei smiled and nodded at George to respond.

"Nous vous entendons haut et fort," George responded.

Beginning in Russian and finishing in English, the Governor General said, "Representatives of the future of humankind. I'd like to say a few words. You are representatives of the world's future. As the station has been flying for so many years with a human on board with no gap, this is a great success. We have been flying and cooperating for a long time. And the teamwork that you demonstrate today is exactly what we should replicate on Earth more often. As the African proverb says, 'If we choose to go alone, we might go fast, but if we go together, we go farther.' And that is what you are doing for us today. Thank you."[1]

She then gave some specific messages to some of the crew members, including George, in French. "George, you are a worthy representative of Canada. Congratulations on your success in arriving at the ISS. Bravo."

George felt a wave of pride and thanked her. It was a source of pride in the Canadian Space Agency that one of their own had been recognized as the Queen's representative to Canada.

Several friends and family of crew members were present and had brief conversations with them during the event. It was all rather strange, since the world was watching. Jean, Kevin, and Nate all had a quick turn at the mic, and George told them it had been a smooth flight and he was enjoying discovering what it was like to be weightless.

The media event finished, and Alexei took them on a tour of the station, and they reviewed emergency procedures.

After a meal with the rest of the crew, Dave and George could finally move their belongings from the Soyuz into their sleep stations. Yuri would sleep in the Soyuz itself until the next crew rotation.

As George secured his personal items in his sleep station, he had a moment of solitude for the first time all day. He could hear Dave unpacking across the aisle in his pod. It felt good to stop for a few minutes. This morning he ate breakfast in Kazakhstan; now he was in orbit on a space station with Russians and Americans. It was amazing what had been achieved to build and maintain this station. The Governor General's speech had been stirring, yet humanistic. Humans, in his opinion, could not accomplish anything. He fully believed they were flawed and needed God. He wondered how those flaws might show up during this mission.

He started up his NASA laptop and checked to see what was on his task list for the rest of the day. He had only one more item to complete, which was to start a handover of the Canadarm2 from Steve, so he left the pod and went in search of him.

George found Steve in the Columbus laboratory. He couldn't get much further away from his sleeping berth, so it gave him an excellent opportunity to practice moving around the station in zero-g without being observed. Which was good because he rocketed into some cabinets with force to start with. It took some practice to estimate how hard to push off to travel through a module, and his aim wasn't very good.

"Ay, Steve, are you busy?"

"Just finishing up a calibration. Are you wanting to talk about the Canadarm?"

"Yep, we can get a start on the handover," said George.

"Sure, I just have a couple of steps to complete here. How was your flight?"

"Amazing. Pretty much as I expected. But I'm glad we could do the short rendezvous. It would be cramped in there if it took 2 days."

"Well, I can attest to that," said Steve. "With all the cargo they put in the orbital module, there's not that much room to move. I was very glad to dock here."

Steve finished his tasks, updated Mission Control, and then they headed to Node 3, also known as Tranquility.

George followed Steve, careful not to move too quickly. He had to execute a left turn from Columbus as they entered Node 2 and moved into the US Lab, full of experimental racks. Then they flew into the Unity module, Node 1 and turned right into Node 3, which contained their space toilet, washroom, exercise equipment and at the end, the Cupola, a multi-window area that afforded 360-degree views around it, as well as views directly to Earth.

"Ok, let's open up the windows so that we can see, and I'll give you a few minutes to gawk!" said Steve.

They worked through the process of opening the protective covers, and then George said, "Wow!"

Below them was the mostly blue Earth with streaks of white clouds and the occasional blob of green or brown land. The sun glinted off the ocean. And then all around them, George could see the ISS modules, truss, and solar panels. And space, a vast nothingness, with uncountable stars visible.

"Breathe," said Steve.

And George realised he had been gaping and not breathing. He took a breath. "That is amazing."

"Yep. The best place in the station, hands down. If you look back over here, you can see the Candarm2 stowed back over on the truss."

George turned around and located the robot arm. One end of the 17 .6-metre arm connected to the Mobile Base System (MBS), which could travel along rails on the main truss of the station. Near it, he could see Dextre, the Special Purpose Dexterous Manipulator, a two-armed robot. NASA or CSA often operated both from the ground, while astronauts would control them during spacewalks or docking procedures from the control station here in the Cupola, or the one in the Destiny Module.

"So the arm is idle at the moment?" asked George.

"Yes, for your docking, and we have exclusive use over the next day. We have some tasks for you to perform tomorrow so that you to get some hands-on experience. You can see all the controls here, but the control station isn't active at the moment."

"Great. How have you found it?"

"I've only used it three or four times. The sim is pretty close to the real thing. But watching the real thing is cool!"

George nodded in agreement, unable to tear his eyes away from the incredible view of the universe around them, contrasted with the starkness of the man-made station. He could hardly believe that he was actually there, in the Cupola, part of something so much bigger than himself. It made him feel so small, yet so alive.

As he gazed out at the stars, a memory from his childhood came to mind. He had been sailing with his family, and they had been out on the water for hours. It had been peaceful and quiet, the only sounds being the wind in the sails and the gentle lapping of the water against the hull of the boat. And as the sun began to set, turning the sky a beautiful shade of pink and orange, George felt a sense of awe wash over him. He had never felt so connected to the world around him, so in tune with the forces that governed his life. It was a moment that had stayed with him, and he had often thought back on it.

"Yup, we all come here and stare out at space when we have a chance," said Steve.

"Sorry, I got lost in the view again," said George. "Did you get a chance to use Dextre, or just the arm itself?"

"I did once, but mostly it's controlled remotely. You'll come up here and look around and see it has moved way across the station carrying something. A bit spooky."

George nodded as he stared out at the vastness of space once more.

---

1. Transcription of actual speech 4 December 2018

10

SUNDAY, 27TH MAY 2018

It had been a busy two weeks since arriving at the ISS, receiving handovers on the Candarm2 and Dextre, and various systems and experiments for which he would be responsible.

Today they had some rest time, and he planned to use some of it talking with his family and some as a sort of devotional time, since he couldn't attend a church service. He'd noticed that he had spent little time praying, reading God's word, and relating to Him over the last month or so with all the activity around the launch, and he wanted to rectify that.

George joined the crew in the Unity Module for breakfast. The Russians brought their meals from the section, while the NASA and CSA crew made theirs in the galley. Meal times were an opportunity to interact and communicate. So much of the time they were often working alone, or with one other person. He believed this would become more pronounced as the crew size shrank to only 3 people when the Expedition 55 crew departed and before their replacements arrived.

"Did you sleep well in, George?" asked Yuri, securing himself against a wall.

"Yes, it was nice to have a lie-in. It seems to have been all 'go' lately," replied George.

"It'll settle down after a while," said Steve.

"What was it like when the previous crew left?" asked George.

"Like taking a breath, then silence," said Yevgeny. "It's busy before they leave, and then after, you are often alone in this tin can."

"It is a lot different with only three of you on the station," said Steve. "It was probably worse for me as the only NASA person here. These guys would be down in the Zvezda watching a Russian movie, and I've got the rest of the station to myself. It took a few days to realise we needed to think more about each other. So don't forget Yuri."

"What do you plan for today, George?" asked Yuri.

"I'm looking forward to talking to my family, and then doing some devotions," said George.

Dave chuckled and rolled his eyes. "Aye, I'll be watching a football match," he said.

Steve smiled at the two of them. "I think I'll be taking some photos from the Cupola today," he said.

Yuri nodded in agreement. "I plan to call my family too," he said with a smile.

"Well, we Russians have decided that we will watch a movie together later this afternoon," Alexei announced with enthusiasm. "We have Legend of Kolovrat, about a medieval knight."

"Hmm, Kolovrat ... Is that 'spinning wheel'?" asked Dave.

"Yes, he uses two swords at once and spins!"

Everyone around the table laughed. It would be nice to have a bit of time away from work and talk about something other than station operations or experiments for once.

After breakfast, everybody dispersed. George wanted some time alone for his devotion and call with his family. The sleep pods were in a central part of the station, which was fairly busy during the day, so he took his laptop and headed down through the Destiny and Harmony modules to the Kibō module, the Japanese laboratory. It had a couple of small windows, and he opened the covers so that he could see outside. It wasn't as good as the cupola, but it gave some connection to the world outside.

A couple of months before he had left, Jean had suggested that they talk with their pastor, Don, about organising some material that George could use during his ISS mission to maintain his Christian faith. George had realised that he had been neglecting his personal reflective time praying and reading the Bible, and together they spoke with Don. George now had a bunch of resources that Don had gathered for him, and they had arranged to email weekly to discuss one topic and even to video conference if possible.

As George stared out of the windows at the stars he could see, he realized he had focused intensely on his work during the last week or so and had barely thought about God. He felt guilty. He knew he shouldn't feel that way, but he did.

He found the resource to use that day. It was based on Psalm 8, which starts

Lord, our Lord, how majestic is your name in all the earth!

You have set your glory in the heavens.[1]

Yes, thought George, he could definitely see God's glory in the heavens. As he read on, he came to verse 3:

When I consider your heavens, the work of your fingers, the moon, and the stars, *which you have set in place, what is mankind that you are mindful of them, human beings that you care for them?*[2]

He did feel humble, but yet proud that man had built the ISS. But what was that compared to what God had done by creating all the stars, the moon, and the Earth he could just see below? Really, what was mankind when you looked at the galaxy beyond the window, and the many galaxies beyond that? Obviously, the writer of the psalm had also felt insignificant gazing at the stars.

That just made the next part of the psalm more amazing:

You have made them a little lower than the angels and crowned them with glory and honor. You made them rulers over the works of your hands; you put everything under their feet.[3]

and it expanded further on that.

Why would an almighty, creator God make so much of man, especially since they were rebellious people who mostly rejected him and could do so much evil? George did struggle with that question. Why not throw mankind out and start again?

Even this week, George had basically forgotten God. How could he be crowned with glory and honor?

He knew the answer, but he needed to be reminded. It was because of God's love. The love that sent the perfect Jesus to die on the cross, to pay the penalty for George's rebellion and make a way for him to be able to relate with God. Surely, God's name was majestic, he thought.

Don had provided some songs for George to listen to, and he played them and reflected on them as he wrote his email to Don, sharing his response. He felt encouraged and closer to Jesus after this time.

As he was finishing the email, his laptop started ringing with a video call from Jean.

"Hi, honey," said George, securing the laptop on some Velcro so his family could see him.

"Hi, George, great to see your face," said Jean.

"Hi Dad," said Nate.

"Nate!, Great to see you, buddy, and morning to you, Kev. Looks like your mum dragged you out of bed!"

"Hi," mumbled Kevin.

"It's a wonderful sunny day down here," said Jean. "I might see if I can get these two out on the boat this afternoon."

"Aww, fresh air and sea spray. That'd be nice. The smell up here takes some getting used to, but I guess I have got used to it."

"Aww, yuck," said Nate.

George chuckled. "It's not that bad, Nate. It just smells a bit like unwashed socks."

Jean laughed. "Well, that's something to look forward to when you get back. But how's everything going up there?"

"Oh, it's going great," replied George. "I'm settling in well, and the guys up here are all great to work with. Everybody is relaxing a bit this morning, and some are going to watch a Russian movie later."

"And how's your work going?" asked Jean.

"It's going well, but it's busy," said George. "The days are busy, but it's satisfying work."

"I'm sure it is. Just make sure you take some time for yourself as well," said Jean.

"I will, don't worry," said George with a smile. "How are things with you guys?"

"Oh, same old, same old," said Jean. "The boys are keeping me busy."

"Nate, how was your creator camp?"

"It was awesome. We got to play with all this tech and made this movie. I learnt about editing and storyboarding. Have you seen it yet?"

"Ahh, no, not yet."

"And he made lots of friends," said Jean.

"Yeah, my friend Alice has a really cool video channel."

"Wow, that's great."

"What about you, Kevin?"

"Just hanging with friends," said Kevin.

"You've got that International Crew summer camp soon, don't you?"

"Yeah, they sent me some reading to do beforehand."

"Great, that starts next week, doesn't it?"

"Yeah."

"Have a great time if we don't talk before then."

"Sure."

"He really is excited," said Jean, rubbing Kevin's head.

"Hey, I can show you the view out the window. Let me add this external camera," said George.

After a couple of minutes, they could see the view.

"Wow, that's beautiful," said Jean.

"I can't see any stars, Dad," said Nate.

"They are hard to see with the station being so bright, since we are in the sun. Just wait a minute, we are about to cross the terminator, that's the change between day and night, so we'll go into shadow," said George.

A minute later the station moved into Earth's shadow.

"There you go, you might be able to see some now, but this isn't the greatest camera! And the Earth is still bright even on the dark side!"

"There's one," said Nate.

"Let me see, I think that might be Jupiter," said George.

He spent a while longer chatting with his family, and giving them a bit of a tour around the part of the station he was in, and talking about his upcoming spacewalk, then they finished the call.

George sat and stared out the window for a while. The time spent talking with Jean and the kids had been great and refreshed him. The time reading his Bible had recharged him. He felt energised. He grabbed his laptop and flew out of the lab, looking for someone to play chess with.

And he needed to find someone to put Goofy. Each time Dave found Goofy somewhere, he let out a girlish scream. It was hilarious.

---

1. Psalm 8:1, NIV

2. Psalm 8:3-4, NIV

3. Psalm 8:5-6, NIV

11

WEDNESDAY, 30TH MAY 2018

The last few days had been busy as George, Dave, and Steve prepared for the spacewalk by George and Dave to install a redundant battery power cable. They had checked out their suits and ensured that they were charged and full of consumables. Dave and George had spent the night in the airlock, pre-breathing 100% oxygen to purge their bodies of nitrogen so that they would not suffer the bends in the lower atmospheric pressure at which the space suits operated. Now they were wearing masks providing them pure oxygen as Steve helped them put on their bulky space suits. The suits were a white, multi-layered fabric; one with some red stripes, the other with blue stripes, and both had United States of America flags on their left shoulder. Featured on each suit's chest was a control panel and display that the astronaut could look down and observe. Each suit comprised a torso with the life support backpack, a waist section, and legs and boots, plus the two arm sections and gloves. Minor adjustments to each section were possible for the wearer.

It was a slow process, and the space limitations of the airlock meant that only one of them at a time could perform the gymnastics of putting on the parts of the suit. Then, with Steve's help, they checked and double-checked seals and system connections. They performed their first leak tests after they were confident that everything was done correctly. Then Steve ensured that all the tools were in the airlock, closed the hatch, and reduced the pressure to 5 psi. The team conducted another leak test. Both suits passed, and the airlock was evacuated of all air, which took some time.

There wasn't much to do sitting in a space suit in an airlock. The suits dated from the early 1980s. They had no visual displays or even audio playback capability. George could either be alone with his thoughts or talk to Dave, Steve, or the ground, all of which was being streamed on NASA TV, so he took some time to review the upcoming walk. He rehearsed the steps he had to perform in his mind. After he finished, Steve came onto the communications and told them they were about halfway through the procedure.

George thought about his family. He had briefly read an email from Jean. She was worried about Kevin. He had become increasingly withdrawn recently. The upcoming sailing camp might help, and he had quickly replied to that extent. It wasn't easy being the partner of an astronaut. He was away so much of the time, leaving Jean to handle most of the parenting. How was Jean coping? She seemed happy enough on their last video call. Their church was helping her out a bit, and in a few weeks, she would take the boys to visit her family in Canada.

"Okay guys, it looks like we are ready," said Steve. "FLIGHT, ISS, the airlock evacuation is complete."

"Thank you, Steve. You are go to open the airlock hatch," said the Mission Control Capcom, Jane Hurst.

Dave went out first and secured his tethers, then George handed him the tools and followed him. He grabbed the handholds and carefully pulled himself through the hatch, carefully avoiding scraping the suit against anything. Twice he needed to backtrack and try again. Moving was much easier once they were outside the station, but then there was just nothing around him. His head spun at the lack of walls and the infinite nothingness in front of him. He took a deep breath and secured his restraint, focussing on the outside of the ISS. He felt calmer and ventured to look out again. The view was stunning; the Earth below them in all its beauty. For a moment, George forgot about the task at hand and just marvelled at the vastness of the universe before him.

Dave handed him a bag of tools, and he connected it to his body restraint tether.

They installed the hatch temperature cover to stop the airlock getting to hot when it was in full sun. Then they conducted their buddy checks, confirming that each other's suits and tethers were properly configured.

"George will lead, and Dave, you have a tool bag to pick up on the way." Jane's voice crackled through the radio in his helmet.

George cleared his mind. It was time to get to work. They had practised this many times in the Neutral Buoyancy Lab, and it was time to put all that training to use. Dave and George moved around each other in delicate choreography, making sure they correctly latched their safety tether, which allowed them to move up to 25 feet from that location.

As they made their way towards the power cable, George's stomach was tense as he realized the significance of the task they were about to complete. Installing a redundant battery power cable might sound like a simple task, but it was crucial for the survival of the space station.

He focused on his work, making sure that he followed the procedures carefully as they made their way towards the target. They were close now, and once they arrived, Dave handed George the tools he needed to get started. The cable was attached to a pallet on the end of the Canadarm2, which Steve was operating. Carefully packed, the cable came out freely as George and Dave pulled it. It was bulky, with additional layers of protection for the harsh solar space environment.

The only sounds he heard was his breathing, the noise of a fan in his suit, and the communications. George hear the thump of his pulse as he concentrated on the task at hand. The success of this mission relied on his focus, and he was determined to see it through to the end.

They located the first socket, and using his pistol grip tool (PGT), an electric screwdriver, he removed the cover, being careful to retain it and the screws. Then Dave handed him the end of the cable, and he carefully oriented the plug and inserted it in the socket.

"How does that look?" he asked Dave.

"Perfect, I hope they are all that easy," Dave replied. In reality, the expansion and contraction that occurred every ninety minutes could slightly warp components.

"Ok, I'll screw that in place." George carefully selected the opposite direction on his PGT and screwed in the four locking screws. He had difficulty getting the first one to capture, but the rest were simple.

"Jane, how are we on the timeline?" asked Dave.

"Well, that took fifteen minutes, so you are right on track," said Jane in Houston.

Dave started making his way five metres along the truss to the next outlet. Steve moved the CandaArm2 slowly in the same direction, and George followed, managing his safety lines and watching the cable unfurl from its pallet. He stopped twice to loop the cable under a securing bracket.

Reaching the new work location, the Candarm2 proceeded a metre or so further so it was out of their way. Dave took hold of the cable and gently pulled it, and they repeated the actions they had performed on the previous socket. George removed the cover and inserted the socket. Every time he used the PGT, he had to hold on to a rail or otherwise brace himself so that he didn't rotate in the opposite direction that the driver was screwing.

"Okay, let's stop for a minute and grab a drink and take a photo," said Dave after they had finished.

"We are coming up on sunset," said Jane.

As George turned to look down the station, they entered the Earth's shadow almost instantaneously. He opened one of his filters on his helmet so he could see more clearly and was rewarded with a glorious view of the Earth below him. He could make out Europe's coastline and the darkness of the Atlantic.

Beads of sweat formed on his forehead. He couldn't do much about them, and hoped the suit's systems would dry the air out soon. "I seem to have worked up a sweat," he said.

"You'll cool down now the sun's gone," said Dave. "I'll do the next one."

First, they had to relocate their safety tethers. Jane gave each of them the locations they were to use for their second safety tether, separated by a few metres, so they hopefully did not get them tangled, then they both translated, using their hands, back along the truss and released their first safety tether, before returning to their new work location.

Once they were there, the Candarm2 had arrived with their cable. This time George held the cable, while Dave inserted the cable socket. By this time, the sun had risen again.

He noticed a small drop of water pass his vision. "Jane, I've just noticed a water droplet in my helmet, and I'm feeling something cold on my neck."

"Copy that, George. Let us know immediately if you see more."

"Copy," said George. He was concerned. There'd been issues in the past with a water leak in some EVA suits. In 2013 Italian astronaut Luca Parmitano experienced a significant water leak into his helmet that had become life-threatening.

"This second bolt does not want to come undone," said Dave.

"You can use PGT setting Bravo two, but you will need to brace yourself," said Jane.

"Copy," said Dave.

A bead of sweat trickled down his forehead. He couldn't afford to panic, but his mind was racing with the possibilities of what could happen if the water leak continued. He tried to focus on the task at hand, helping Dave with the stubborn bolt.

"Got it!" Dave exclaimed triumphantly as the bolt finally loosened.

George let out a sigh of relief and then saw another water droplet floating in his helmet. "Jane, the droplets are increasing. I think we have a leak."

"Copy, George. Standby," Jane replied.

"Let me have a look," said Dave, bringing his helmet shield to almost touch George's.

George felt a pool of water creep into his ear. "There's water in my ear."

"Yes, I see that," said Dave.

"We see it too on the cameras," said Jane. "We want you both to return to the airlock. Leave your tools tethered where they are."

"Copy that," said Dave and George.

George disconnected his local tether, as droplets continued to form in his helmet, obscuring his vision. The fear that had been gnawing at George's gut suddenly exploded. He controlled his breathing as he had been trained. Panicking now would not help. He prayed silently for God's help as he navigated along the truss to the next tether point. Dave followed behind, and when George was secure, disconnected George's safety tether and came to him.

"How are you going, George?" asked Dave.

"It's not too bad, but I've got water in my right eye." In zero-g, water forms balls, and surface tension means it spreads over the object it touches. There was now a small puddle around his eye. He did not want any water to enter his nose or mouth when he was breathing. Although at least he could swallow it if it got into his mouth.

Jane gave them directions to continue their translation to the airlock. Fortunately, they had previously staged retractable tethers which allowed them to safely progress from this point to the airlock with no need to connect new tethers.

"Okay Jane, we've reached Papa 1-962," said Dave.

"You need to go nadir until the next junction, Dave," said Jane. Nadir was the part of the station pointing to the Earth.

"Copy," said Dave.

"And we have some precautions for you. Avoid the power cables on your right."

"Copy. Okay George, can you see the rail in front of you heading off away from us?"

"Yep," replied George.

"Great, follow that."

George could make out the rail, and he grasped it in one hand, and carefully twisted his body around so his torso was above him, and began translating along the rail.

"You are looking good there," said Dave. "I'm right beside you. You're clear of the hazards," said Dave.

"Ok," said George. A drop of water ran up his nose. He blew out sharply to dislodge it, but it didn't move easily. With a bit more success, he tried again. He really wanted a cloth to wipe his face. It was totally different to how water behaved on Earth. It clung to surfaces, so it was spreading around his nose. "I've got some water in my nose."

"Ok, buddy, hang in there," said Dave. "Jane, we are just at the next junction."

"Great, head starboard to Sierra 0-010. You should have a clear run. There are power cables to avoid nadir of your path."

"Copy that. Dave, that's the rail just to your right."

"Okay, I'll just swing around. Whoa, a big glob of water just went past and stuck on my visor."

"Okay, I'm going to attach my working tether to you, and haul you, ok?"

"It's okay with me if it's okay with Jane."

"We are happy with that," said Jane.

Dave connected up his tether to George, and then quickly hauled them both along the rail. “Any issues with our tethers before we get to the airlock, Jane?”

“No, they are all clear.”

“Copy that, then I intend to traverse using our usual path straight to the airlock.”

“We concur,” said Jane.

“I’m at the airlock controls ready for you guys,” said Steve.

“We are going to slow down and turn here, George,” said Dave.

“Yup, I’m trying to keep orientated so the water stays away from my face.”

“How’s that going?”

“Not that well, you bounce a lot! Pffh, water in my mouth.”

“Okay, turning now, not that far. Just need to cross Sierra 0. And we are onto Node 1 now.”

“Great.” George felt water spread across his face.

“Just grab that rail, I’ll tether you there, green tether to November 1330. OK, let me get this cover open.”

“Guys, you are doing well. Dave tether yourself, please. Blue to November 1332.”

“Copy that, blue to November 1332, done.”

“Great,” said Jane. “Also for George blue to November 1331.”

“Copy, done.”

“And finally, for you green to November 1331.”

“Also done.”

“Continue opening the airlock heat shield, Dave.”

“Ok, I’m glad we didn’t secure this too tight.” Dave undid a bolt securing the heat shield and folded it up.

“You are ‘go’ to open the airlock hatch, Dave,” said Jane.

“Opening the hatch,” said Dave. It swung in.

“Ingress George first, remove his blue tether,” said Jane.

“Copy, George first, remove blue tether. Are you able to swing your feet in, George?”

“Sure, Dave.” George levered himself so his feet started entering the airlock hatch. He managed to enter properly the first time and found a hook and tethered himself inside. “Ok, I’m tethered in here.”

“Dave, go ahead and remove George’s green tether. George, wait for Dave before removing your tool bag given your lack of visibility.”

“Okay,” said George.

“Copy,” said Dave.

“And, Dave, you can begin your ingress. Please remember to attach the magnetic hook to the thermal cover.

“Yup, removing my blue tether. You in, George? Or I’ll kick you in the head.”

“I’m in as far as I can, but I can’t see much. Water up my nose, too.”

“Ok. If this cover would just stay still. I’ll hook it up ... okay, done. I’m ingressing now.” Dave pulled himself into the airlock, past the hatch.

“Okay Dave, when you are ready, please close the hatch,” said Jane.

“Copy, that, closing the hatch.” Dave swung the hatch closed and spun the handle to lock it. “Hatch is closed.”

“Copy that we are seeing a good lock. Dave, please connect George’s power and pressurization hoses.”

“Okay, I just have to get his tool bag out of the way.”

“George, how are you going?” asked Jane.

“Ok, I’ve got the tool bag out of the way. Hooking up his O2 hose.”

“George, how do you read?” said Jane.

“I don’t think he can hear you,” said Dave. “George, squeeze my hand if you can hear me. George, can you hear me. Jane, I don’t think he can hear me, but he looks okay — miserable, but okay.”

"Okay, thanks, Dave. Steve, you are go to begin expedited pressurisation."

The team worked to quickly pressurise the airlock.

George was concerned that he couldn't hear the communications, but he could see the activity that Dave was undertaking, or at least he could see some of it. He had to calm himself. He did not want to drown in space!

After a few minutes Steve reported that the air pressure had equalised, and the crew worked to open the airlock hatch from the equipment lock, and then moved George into that area. Houston allowed them to skip some checklist items to quickly get George out of his suit, and once his helmet was off, they quickly used towels to mop up the water.

"Hi Dave, had a bit of a swim, eh?" said Steve.

"I am glad to see you guys," said George. "Thanks for the towel dry."

"Hey guys, I'm going to hardline my suit. How's George going?"

"Okay, Dave, we copy that. They've got George's helmet off and he is doing ok."

"Yep, that's okay. I'll just hang out back here until they are ready for me."

George relaxed while Steve, Yuri, Yevgeny and Alexi, worked around him to remove his suit. He was glad to be able to breathe easily once again.

"Can you guys see where the leak was?" he asked.

"Not really," said Steve. "There's water everywhere. I wouldn't be surprised if it's the sublimator again."

"Shit," said George, "this probably cancels the rest of the EVAs for this mission."

"Yeah, that is bad for you guys. I had no problems with that suit a couple of months ago," said Steve. "Okay, we've finished the checklist on your suit, so we'll get the torso off you and then we'll work on Dave."

That pulled George out of his dispirited mood. Dave was still floating around in the airlock in his suit. "Right, tell me what you want to do."

"How about you get changed first? We can handle Dave."

"Okay, I'll be back soon."

George pushed himself out of the equipment lock into Node 1 and across into Node 3 which contains the bathroom. He grabbed a fresh towel and finished drying his hair. Then he went back into Node 1, saw that the team had Dave's visor open, and then went through the US Lab (Destiny) and into Node 2 where his sleep station was located. He quickly changed into his normal work clothes, and then went back to Node 1. The team had already removed Dave's Safer, the rescue device used if an space walker got separated from the ISS, and his helmet, and were currently working on removing his gloves and suit arms.

"Okay, what do you want me to do, Steve?"

"We have enough people here. Mission Control wants to talk to you on two. They've already chased me up twice about that, so can you chat to them in Destiny. Thanks," said Steve.

"Oh okay, if you are sure. I'll go have a chat with Capcom." He then went back to Destiny and selected the second communications channel.

George's voice was strained as he spoke into his comms, "Hi FLIGHT. This is George, on Two."

"George, this is Jane. How are you feeling?"

"I'm feeling great," said George with a forced chuckle. "Especially now I'm not trying to breathe through water!"

Jane's voice quietened, her concern palpable. "So the doc wanted to know if you'd breathed in any water?"

"No, I didn't have any problem there."

"That's good. So, when did you first notice the water?" asked Jane.

"Just before I said something on comms. I just felt the cold water on my neck."

"So, there'd been no sign before that?"

"No, there had been nothing wrong with the suit. Everything had been working fine. The temperatures were all okay," George replied quickly.

"Also, the team wants to know if you've used any nonstandard hygiene products today."

"Ahh, negative, I've only been using the standard items."

Jane's voice shook a little as she spoke next. "Okay, I guess you realise that this probably means we won't be able to conduct the next EVA, or finish this one. We're very sorry about that. There'll be an investigation into that suit, and we'll probably be bringing it back on one of the next Dragon cargo flights. There's one scheduled for June, so we will try and add a replacement suit to its manifest."

George's composure cracked. "Yes, I was expecting that. I guess that means that I won't get any more EVAs on this mission."

"I'm afraid that's likely to be the case, although you might get one when the next crew arrives," said Jane hesitantly, her words loaded with sombre finality. "I expect they will be deemed only to be used in emergencies."

"That's a pain", George muttered bitterly, his voice trailing off into bitter silence.

"That's all we've got for you now. I'm sure there will be some questions coming from the team for you later, so watch your email. Thanks, George."

"Okay , thanks, Jane. Clear on two."

George hung up the microphone.

"George, good to see you safe," said Dave as he came out of the equipment lock.

"Thanks, and thank you for hauling me back to the airlock. That was getting scary."

"You'd do the same for me. That would have been freaky."

"It was not fun. I thought they'd got a handle on the issue, but it seems not. Jane was just telling me they will likely cancel this EVA, not sure about the next. The suits will be emergency use only."

"You're kidding, there goes all the training we did," said Dave. He sighed, "I understand why, but that is really disappointing since they were our primary mission objectives."

"I know, right?"

"Listen, give me ten minutes to clean up, then we can go through the post-EVA checklists on those suits, and anything else Mission Control wants us to do."

"Sure."

George slowly pushed himself to the kitchen to get a snack. Was it worth all the effort to come here?

12

Friday, 1st June 2018

George checked the checklist again. Yes, he had read correctly. He had to remove the window in the experiment and clean the glass. Here he was, one of the most highly trained Canadians on the planet, in orbit of the Earth at great expense, cleaning a window! Apparently, it was an important window, or it wouldn't be on his checklist, but still, he was a window cleaner.

He had received official confirmation that morning. The EVA suits were a no-go for normal operations, and a replacement for his suit would be shipped on a future cargo flight, and his would be returned to the ground for testing.

He sighed and opened the box that held the cleaning supplies. Pulling out a soft cloth and some special cleaning solution, he followed the instructions carefully. He sprayed the cloth with a generous amount of solution before gently wiping down the surface of the window. Carefully ensuring he used circular motions to avoid smears on the glass, his patience was rewarded as he saw it clear before his eyes.

Using a clean cloth dampened in deionized water, he wiped down any residual cleaner that remained. Finally, satisfied with his work, George put away all of his tools and reported to mission FLIGHT that his task was complete.

George returned to his sleep station. A call was scheduled with Jean, so he wanted somewhere private. The rest of the crew were scattered around the station, with Dave and Steve in the Japanese lab, while the Russians were all in their section.

He set up the call on his 'personal' laptop to Jean. He might get video if there was enough bandwidth available, but since they would be out of range of the Tracking and Data Relay Satellites (TRDS) at times, his video would drop out occasionally.

"Hi, George, how are you?" asked Jean as she answered the call, settling into her seat in front of the camera.

"Jean, it's so good to see you. I'm okay, just a bit annoyed at being a window washer today."

"What?"

"I just finished a task cleaning a window on an experiment. Just me grumbling. How are you?"

"I'm okay. It's been a busy morning. Nate and I are taking a couple of his friends, and one of their dads, out for a sail this afternoon, so I've been preparing some food."

"Aww, that sounds fun. I wish I were there."

"So do I, but you've been wanting this mission for years."

"Yeah, but I just lost a big chunk of it. No spacewalks, at least until we can get another suit up here, which will be at least 2 months."

"That's good, so you still may get to do the EVAs."

"Maybe."

Jean smiled sympathetically at him. "I know it's not the same as if everything had gone according to plan, but you're still in space and you're still doing important work up there. And you'll have plenty of opportunities to make up for this later on."

George sighed, "Yeah, I know. It's just frustrating, you know?"

"I get it. But think about all the amazing things you've already accomplished. And you're surrounded by a team of brilliant people."

He smiled gratefully at her. "Thank you, Jean. You always know how to cheer me up."

"That's my wifely duty," she teased.

They talked for a little while longer, catching up on all the little things that had happened in their lives since George had gone into space. As they were saying their goodbyes, a warning alarm warbled in the station. He abruptly ended the call and hurried to the nearby Caution and Warning System Panel in Node 2. It confirmed it was a warning! He looked at the nearby command control laptop and noted a power condition.

"FLIGHT, this is George on one in Node 2."

"Go ahead, George."

"We have a power system warning up here."

"Copy that, we see that. It was an unexpected alert related to some battery charging work the team is doing. At this time, please acknowledge the alert and the team here will review."

"Copy, acknowledging and nothing more for us to do."

"Correct. FLIGHT is clear."

"Anything to worry about?"

"No, Steve, just a power system alert, triggered by ground team work."

"Cool. Are you okay?"

"Yep, just my first alarm since I've been here."

"Wow, must have been a quiet period!"

"I guess. I better let Jean know everything is alright since I scampered out of a call with her."

Steve smiled. They'd all been there.

George went back to his sleep station and wrote a quick email to Jean explaining what had happened. It was just another part of life on the ISS.

13

MONDAY, 9TH JULY 2018

The last month had been tedious for George. Sure, he was in space, but after a while, the novelty wore off. A lot of the day-to-day work was maintenance, cleaning, and working on experiments. He'd missed his big-ticket item, the spacewalks. His suit was to go back on the next cargo flight, which would bring up a replacement suit. There wasn't even that much he needed to do with Candarm2 since it was mostly remote-controlled. This disappointment, combined with missing out on the Artemis 2 mission, had led to a general funk.

Jean and his team had been trying to encourage him, but Dave was also disappointed. George was missing his family and friends, and church. He'd become less regular in his devotion times with God, and had spent a lot of time staring out the windows when he had the opportunity.

So it wasn't a surprise to Dave to find George in the cupola with a camera in hand, staring out at the view. It was a common place for crew to go during downtime. In fact, all the crew had received additional training so they could take good photos.

"Buddy, what are we looking at?" asked Dave.

"I think even you can identify Australia, mate."

"Yep, you're right. I can do so. Anywhere you've been?"

"I think we can see Broome. We did a trip to Western Australia once and visited there. The distances are vast, like we have in Canada, and we spent most of our time on the East Coast."

"There's not a lot there," said Dave.

"Nope, it's a small town, but very multicultural. A lot of pearl diving happened there. But we were only there for two days."

"Was that just you and Jean?"

"Kevin was with us, but very young."

"I guess you miss them."

"Yeah, I do wonder whether its worth being up here and away from them so long."

"Isn't this what you told me God wanted you to do?"

"Yeah, but I didn't expect to be a space janitor."

"Come on, we do more than cleaning. You're doing science every day."

"Yeah, but most of the time I don't know or understand what is going on," said George.

"True, but sometimes you do, and there are some cool experiments going on up here."

"I guess it's just not what I expected."

"So God does get things wrong!"

"It seems so," said George.

"Right. Come on, we are having a movie night, and I've got just the movie - Mad Max!"

"I'll pass, thanks."

"No, you don't get the option. We need some escapism for a while, and crazy Aussies driving around fuel trucks in a post-apocalyptic desert seems good to me."

14

TUESDAY, 17TH JULY 2018

An unwavering alarm tone sounded in the ISS.

George quickly checked the nearby Caution and Warning System Panel. 'ATM' was lit, which suggested an atmosphere contamination. He checked the the control laptop for the type of warning and saw that it was a possible ammonia leak.

"FLIGHT, this is George on one in Node 2."

"Go ahead, George."

"We have an emergency alarm for a potential ammonia leak."

"Copy that, George. We advise you to don masks, and we will get back to you shortly."

"What's happening, George?" asked Dave, who was station commander after the previous crew had left the week before.

"Dave, it looks like there's a possible ammonia leak. Mission Control is checking now. They want us in breathing masks."

Dave opened a cabinet and removed two breathing apparatuses stored there, handing one to George.

"George, can you grab a couple of day's rations in case we need to spend some time in the Russian segment?"

"Sure."

"Station, this is FLIGHT on One."

George handed Dave the microphone, just as Yuri appeared from the US Lab segment wearing a gas mask.

"This is Dave, go ahead."

"Dave, we'd like you to evacuate to the Russian segment. Initiate the Ammonia Release Response. Disconnect the ventilation hoses and seal the hatch while we work this issue."

"Copy that, evac to the Russian segment."

All three men headed back through the US Lab and into Node 1.

"George can you disconnect the ventilation duct? Yuri, we'll need to clone the NODE 1 aft hatch to the PMA."

All three entered the Pressurized Mating Adapter joining the US and Russian segments, and sealed it off.

"Okay guys, all three of us are here. Since we were all in there, we all need to doff our clothes and leave them in the PMA. That's what the emergency clothes in there are for," said Dave.

They all quickly got out of the clothes they were wearing in case they had absorbed any ammonia, bagged them and put on the clothes stored there, entered the FSB in the Russian Segment and then sealed the PMA hatch.

"I'll get the masks and kits," said Yuri. He went a cabinet and retrieved three ammonia measurement its and emergency masks which were designed to filter out ammonia.

"I'll conduct the tests here. Yuri, you conduct the test in the Soyuz and activate it, and George, test in Zarya and Zvezda and I'll test in the MLM. Call your results to ground," said Dave.

George pushed off into the Russian segment, into the Zarya module. He performed a test there. No ammonia was recorded. He flew along into the Zvezda module and ran another test.

"STATION this is FLIGHT," same the voice over the radio.

George could hear Dave say, "FLIGHT, STATION, go ahead."

"Dave, we have shutdown cooling loop 1, which showed a slight pressure drop. We are in the process of shutting down nonessential systems. Have you got any test results?"

"Ahh, outside the PMA hatch I'm reading 3 ppm, which is good. I hadn't smelt anything before the alarm," said Dave.

"That's good. The readings we have seen are also low."

"FLIGHT, this is George. My tests are not registering any ammonia in Zarya and Zvezda."

"Copy that, George," said Mission Control.

"FLIGHT, this is Yuri, in the Soyuz. I've started the activation sequence. Tests show no ammonia."

"Copy that, Yuri. Please, all proceed to the Soyuz and we will test again in 30 minutes."

"Copy that," said Dave.

George headed back toward the Zarya module, and Dave appeared. "After you," said George.

Dave, then George, floated down to their Soyuz, opening the hatch, entering, and closing the hatch behind them.

"Ahh, the merry band is back in their home, yes?" said Yuri.

"Hopefully it's not a long stay", said George. Although they had removed the cargo they had carried up, it had already been replaced by rubbish that would burn up with the service modules on their return, so it was cramped inside.

"Are there cards in here somewhere?" asked Dave.

"I know where they are," said George, opening a cabinet and pulling out a pack.

Dave took the communications microphone and said, "FLIGHT, Soyuz, we are all in the capsule now and sealed off."

"Copy that, Dave. We'll give you a call in about twenty-five minutes to perform another round of tests. If your tests in the capsule are still below three, you can remove your masks."

"Copy that, we will test again," said Dave. He looked at Yuri, who started another test, and returned to his startup checklist, getting the module's life support active.

With Yuri operating from the middle seat, it was easier for Dave and George to float around in the orbital module.

"You guys brought some with you. We got 1 ppm, so it's safe to doff our masks," said Yuri. "FLIGHT, we measured 1 part per million, so we are removing our masks."

"What do you guys want to play?" asked Dave, shuffling the cards.

"Don't you need to be commanding or something?" said George.

"Nothing to do. Yuri is getting the ship up and running, FLIGHT is dealing with our problem, and my job is to entertain you. What are we playing?"

"Gin rummy?"

"Sure. Yuri, do yo want in on the first hand or are you still doing the checklist?"

"I'll be ten minutes, easy," said Yuri from the cockpit.

"George, find us something to deal onto. There has to be a clipboard of something around," said Dave.

George started looking in lockers. He moved a flight suit out of the way. "You know, it'd be a bummer if we had to go home now, just when we get the replacement suit next week with the new crew."

"Not an issue. This is a small leak. Once they've dispersed it in the US section, we'll be back in there tomorrow, if not today," said Dave.

"But we might be down to one cooling loop," said George.

"A few science racks will have to be shutdown, but we'll still get our walk. Where's your faith, buddy?"

"AWOL, apparently." George moved another flight suit out of the way so that he could look in another locker.

"We've had a few setbacks, but we're trained for that. Our walk will probably happen, perhaps just one, but I think they are working to include a second one. We might go home a few days later if the logistics will work."

"Here we are, hopefully this will do," said Dave, pulling out a small board with multiple straps on it.

"See, you are trained to do this! Now I need a third hand to deal my hand to." The solution, as usual, was for Dave to deal both hands into George's hands. Once they'd sorted out the deck, they started playing.

"Right," said Yuri floating through the hatch, "you can deal me in now."

Dave sighed. "Give me your cards, George. We'll start again."

Twenty minutes later, Mission Control called them and asked that they perform more checks in the Russian segment, so then donned their masks, opened the hatch, and Dave floated off to test the air in different parts of the Russian part of the station. George closed the hatch behind him.

"So you are struggling, George eh?" said Yuri.

"I don't know if I'd say struggling."

"No," said Yuri , raising his hand. "It is disappointing when important things don't happen. Lots of training we do, and sometimes we never use it. For my first visit to ISS I spent six months training on the process to install protection panels on Zarya. It was before we started training in a more general manner for spacewalks. I could do the process blindfolded. In fact, they did blindfold me. When I got up here, they changed to spacewalk. I had to run cables. I didn't know how to run cables. They had trained me to place panels. Uvy. We have to learn not to get too attached to what we think we will do. Look," he said, pointing to a window. "We are in space orbiting the Earth."

"I know this Yuri, but it's still hard."

"And you didn't get to go on your moon shot. Maybe you get to walk on it? Eh?"

"FLIGHT, STATION, I have test results," said Dave over the communications system.

"STATION, go ahead, Dave."

"Tests in both Zarya and Zvezda are 2 ppm."

"Copy that, standby STATION."

"We should be able to go out," said George.

"Good. Even I don't like being cramped up in there," said Yuri.

"STATION, FLIGHT. You are free to move around in the Russian segment without your masks. We are still working through data from the cooling loops and we will have a plan for you shortly."

"Copy that," said Dave.

"FLIGHT, SOYUZ, we are opening our hatch and powering down."

"Copy that, Yuri."

George opened the hatch and tied it back, fetching the ventilation tube from the docking area. He fed it down into the Soyuz capsule itself to give Yuri fresh air and cooling.

"Yuri, I'll go back and see if Dave wants a hand if you are right there."

"Shutdown is quicker. I'll join you in 5 minutes," said Yuri.

George found Dave at the command center.

"The results don't look too bad," said Dave. "I think we'll be able to go back inside in a couple of hours."

"Great," said George. "Have they given us any tasks on our job sheets?"

"Not yet. It's almost lunch, so I reckon we eat, and they might have a plan for us by the time we've finished."

An hour later, Mission Control did indeed have a plan. Dave and George again powered off the ventilation fans, and while wearing the special ammonia respirators, they opened the PMA hatch into Node 1 and tested for ammonia in each of the modules. There were low positive readings in all the modules, with slightly higher readings in Node 2. They returned to the PSA, closed the hatch and restarted the fans and consulted with Mission Control, who repeated the process in another hour. So after helping Yuri with some cleaning activities, they repeated the process. This time Mission Control was happy, and they could restart the ventilation fans, keep the hatch open, and reconnect ventilation hoses.

How would the station operate with only half its cooling?

15

THURSDAY 26TH JULY 2018

Fortunately, the station's design allowed it to operate on just one cooling loop, even though they had to power down many of the science racks.

It was deemed safe to launch the next crew, who had arrived on Tuesday. To keep the crew busy a cargo vessel had arrived on Wednesday, which included the replacement space suit. The American space suits would not fit in a Soyuz, so it had to be shipped separately. Most of the unpacking activities had been delayed to allow for Dave and George's space walk.

The new crew consisted of commander Viktor Belinsky, flight engineer Natalya Solovyova, and NASA mission specialist Caleb "Vance" Sterling. Viktor and Natalya were working on unpacking critical items, while Vance and Yuri worked with Dave and George, who undertook their space walk.

Yuri opened the airlock's internal hatch and waved at George and Dave. George had a huge smile on his face. He found the relevant cables and hoses and connected each of them to the ISS systems. "Welcome back spacewalkers," he said on the communication channel, "You look happy, George."

"I'm tired, but happy that we completed that walk. We may not get another, but we got well into the second walk's objectives," said George.

"And you didn't have to almost drown in the process," said Dave. "That was a long day. Come on, Yuri, stop yapping and get these helmets off."

Vance flew into the airlock and joined Yuri in working through the checklists to make their spacesuits safe and open the helmets. About five minutes later, they could remove their helmets and were given some snacks.

"That's better," said Dave. "I'm starving. I'll take another one of those bars, thanks."

"Wow, I thought you were going to float off when that cable slipped while you were tightening it," said George.

"That's why we have two restraints! But it's not fun hitting their limits."

"I'm sure it made a good video and will be all over the socials," said George.

"Ha," said Dave.

"Are you happy to go home now, George?" asked Yuri.

"Who ever wants to leave the ISS? But yes, we can go home and see our families. Just promise to bring me back one day."

16

Saturday 28th July 22018

The burnt-orange glow of plasma engulfed the Soyuz capsule as the crew plummeted back to Kazakhstan. George was buffeted around in his seat. They had separated from the living section and service module forty minutes earlier. Now they were pressed into their seats, feeling four times their normal weight as the energy the launch imparted to them literally burnt off, as the atmosphere slowed them down to a suborbital speed.

The plasma glow engulfed the cabin. Out of the window he could see streams in it, brighter patches, coming and going. It was amazing the plasma didn't burn away the window!

After a few minutes, the glowing stopped as they slowed down.

"We are coming up on drogue chute release in two minutes. That will be pretty violent, so remember to keep your arms in close and hold on to any items," said Yuri.

"Are we on track?" asked George. The noise of air rushing against the spacecraft was getting louder.

"So far, we are nominal," said Yuri. "Brace!"

There was a bang, the craft shook a little, then there was a little bit of kick followed by a sharp jolt as the chute deployed and the capsule swung in every direction at once, or so it seemed. George struggled to keep his arms close.

"Yahoo!" cried Dave.

"You pilots enjoy strange things," said George.

It took about half a minute to settle down.

"Okay, the main chute release is deploying in a minute. That will be much calmer."

"Sure," said George.

A minute later, there was another pop as the main parachute was released and then a bump as it unfurled.

"Main chute deployed," said Yuri.

"Yahoo, we're going to make it," said George.

"Did you doubt?" asked Yuri. "Shield release in 5, 4, 3, 2, 1."

The heat shield and external window covers blew off with a pop.

"Venting started," said Dave, as excess fuel and oxygen was vented.

A helicopter was briefly visible out of one window.

"Good, the cavalry is here," said Dave, "which means we were on target."

Dave and Yuri went through some checklist items, and then Yuri said, "Prepare for landing."

George pulled his arms in tight across his chest, under his chin. All the chairs suddenly popped up to prepare for the landing, and the craft swayed as the parachute orientation changed. They couldn't talk in case they bit their tongues during the 'soft landing'. There was a violent explosion and shock as retro jets fired, their chairs slid back, and George thought he had been in a car wreck.

"Welcome home to Earth," said Yuri. They all cheered and slapped gloved hands.

George could hear voices outside as the recovery team worked to open the hatch. Raising his arm was an effort.

"This gravity is a bitch," said Dave as he lay back down after trying to sit up.

"Did you forget your training?" asked George.

"Apparently, and you'd think I would have learnt the first time."

"It's good we are upright and that the capsule didn't roll. My first landing, we were upside down," said Yuri.

"That would suck," said Dave.

After about ten minutes, the recovery team opened the hatch. The first recovery team member entered the capsule and helped Dave, who was in the center seat, out. Somehow another person fitted in the capsule and the two of them lifted him through the hatch onto a stretcher.

George was next. He avoided eye contact as the team picked him up, but the suit and their loss of condition after zero-g for a few months meant there was little he could do. Soon the brilliant Kazak sun blazed on him, the air was fresh, and he received hand slaps from the ground team. The medical team checked him out and gave him some fluids, and he could recline on the stretcher.

They hauled Yuri out and placed him on a stretcher. As soon as the team was on level ground, Anna, Yuri's wife, was there kissing him and holding his hand. Much more informal than NASA landings.

Medical personnel assessed and helped them change into flight suits before they were loaded onto Roscosmos Mi-8 helicopters.

The helicopter landed in Karaganda. Officials assisted the crew members as they walked from the helicopter to a waiting car. They then drove the crew members to the airport arrivals area. There, officials greeted them, gave them Kazakh cloaks and hats, and presented them with Russian dolls painted with their faces as gifts. Finally, the crew members did press events.

What seemed like an eternity later, the crew had a few minutes alone. Almost, Yuri's wife was with them.

"Yuri, you are so lucky Anna can go to the landing site," said George. "That doesn't happen in the US."

"Yes, it is a bit of a, how you say, dog's breakfast, at the landing. People everywhere, even press," said Yuri. "But yes, we can have family there, at least partners."

"I'm glad we have finished with the press. I'm looking forward to some shuteye on our flight home," said Dave.

"Yeah, this gravity is tiring," said George.

"You need a good rest now. We all did well on the mission. I'm proud of you. We handled problems well, and we are all healthy," said Yuri.

"Thankyou for being our Soyuz commander, Yuri, and Dave, thankyou for commanding the mission," said George.

"As Yuri said, we all did well, and we had some gnarly problems to deal with. We almost finished our mission objectives. I really enjoyed working with you both," said Dave.

A door opened on the far side of the room. "It looks like our flight is ready. Yuri, it's been great to work with you. I hope we get a face to face debrief soon," continued Dave, shaking Yuri's hand and giving him a clap on the shoulder, which Yuri turned into a hug.

"You have done well as commander," said Yuri. "I hope to see you soon. Anna and I will bring Sasha out to Disney World. Maybe Kevin and Nate can come visit? And Juliet?"

"I'm sure they'd love that," said George. "Thank you, and I look forward to seeing you again." He shook Yuri's hand and got a bear hug too.

Dave and George turned and plodded through the door, out to the waiting NASA Gulfstream that would fly them to Houston.

17

Twenty-four hours later, after a refuelling stop in Frankfurt, Dave, and George arrived at Ellington Field, NASA's airfield near Johnston Space Centre.

Jean, Nate, and Kevin, together with Dave's daughter Juliet, were waiting for them at the bottom of the airstairs. George descended the stairs gingerly, his head still didn't agree that the sky was up,, and gathered his family in an embrace.

"Dad, did you fly in space?" said Nate.

"In a capsule, yes," said George, lifting him up in a hug. "Oh, you've grown."

"Yes, a quarter of an inch," said Nate, proudly.

"And how are you going, Kevin."

"Good. I'm glad you're back."

George smiled, "And I'm glad to see you too."

He turned and hugged and kissed Jean. "It's been so long since I held you," he said.

"I'm looking forward to you holding me more," said Jean with a wink.

Roger Glenn, NASA's Chief Astronaut, walked over to them. Dave and Juliet joined them. "Congratulations, both of you, on a great mission. You handled yourselves well, even when things went awry. You have done your nations proud. Come see me next week, and we'll talk about plans for the future. George, I think you'll be really pleased at what we've got planned for you!"

"Thank you, sir," said Dave and George in unison.

"I can see you both need to spend time with your families. Go home and rest. I'm sure your teams will be in touch. Oh, you probably need to talk to the press first!"

After another press briefing, the family all got into their SUV, with Jean driving.

"What do you think Roger was talking about?" asked Jean as she pulled out of the parking space.

"I hope it's Artemis 3," said George.

"What's that, Dad?" asked Nate.

"The moon landing!"

Artemis 3

Firmament Books

—•—

1

Mike Trellis didn't know he was going to make history during his lunar mission, Artemis 3. That was his fellow astronaut Sue Bright's role as the first woman to walk on the moon just five days ago. He wasn't even supposed to be on the mission. He was originally the backup scientist for the mission until George Scorby was diagnosed with thyroid cancer.

Mike and Sue worked through the now very familiar process of preparing for their fourth EVA on the moon. They prepared their xEMUs (Exploration Extravehicular Mobility Unit), each cross-checking their work and assisting each other in donning the suits, all the time careful not to accidentally launch themselves into the ceiling of the lander in the low gravity environment.

Mike easily lifted himself up and through the hatch on the back of the suit. In zero-G, he had stretched from his normal six-foot frame to six-foot-one, so on the moon, he was somewhere in between. The xEMUs had been designed to accommodate a wide range of body types and accommodated his fit but average build.

Sue was likewise an average build, five-foot-four (on earth). She had had long black hair until astronaut training when she needed to shorten it to shoulder length for practical reasons.

As they depressurized the airlock, they each checked their xEMU systems to ensure there were no leaks and that the systems were operating correctly. Mike could feel his pulse and breathing rate rise slightly. This part of the mission was one of the riskier yet most exciting as they explored places no human had been. If something went wrong, there was only one other person here to help. A robotic device might be able to assist, but they were very much alone out here.

2

Wednesday, May 17, 2017

Today was the day of 'The Call'. Mike was expecting it sometime this morning, which made focussing on his work as part of the JPL Mars Science Laboratory Curiosity Rover team difficult. As a member of the geoscience team, he was involved in planning the next activities of the rover during the morning and then reviewing the results of the science experiments in the afternoon. It took all of his concentration to follow the morning discussion regarding Curiosity's operations. It was currently driving towards Vera Rubin Ridge. At least he wasn't the lead today.

This was the second time he had applied to become an astronaut candidate with NASA. Each time more people applied, reportedly 18,000 this time. That he was even part of the shortlist was a miracle. He hadn't even finished his PhD for his first application, but he had interned with the JPL Mars team.

Mike had grown up watching Space Shuttle missions on NASA TV. He'd been captivated by the thought of exploring outer space. His father, John, a software developer, had been in elementary school during the Apollo program and had nurtured Mike's interest. They often watched TV launches together and even trekked from their home in Colorado Springs to Florida's Space Coast to watch the launch of USS Discovery in August 2001.

Throughout school he'd been fascinated by science, especially understanding how the earth and other planets had formed. Mike had been single-minded in his desire to become an astronaut. He'd attended Space Academy during Junior High and later the Advanced Space Academy, building some long-term friendships.

He had decided to study for a Bachelor's degree in Geological and Environmental Sciences at Stanford University, California. After graduating, he studied for a Doctorate in Geology from the University of California, Los Angeles, taking as many opportunities as possible to undertake research on NASA projects, including internships at JPL.

It had been disappointing to receive a letter informing him that he had been unsuccessful as a candidate in 2013. But he had at least gotten past the first cut and had an interview with the Astronaut Selection Board. This time he'd made it much further, with a physical, more interviews and some team activities.

"So, Mike, are you happy with that plan?" asked Georgie, today's Mission lead.

Startled from his thoughts, Mike nodded, "Ahh, that's fine." Fortunately, he didn't have any serious interest in the activities planned for the day. The priority was driving at the moment, but visibility reduced the drive distances that could be planned to around 50 metres, so there were many additional opportunities for additional science.

"That's great. I'll pass the plan on to the engineering team. Data from Sol 1699 should be available this afternoon."

The team all stood and started filing out of the meeting room. As Mike got to the door, he felt his phone vibrate. His pulse began to race as he looked at the number, calming down as he saw his girlfriend's number.

"Hi, Emily, what's up?"

"Hi, I just wanted to check if you were right to go to Jane and Karl's tonight?"

"Ahh – sure, should be ok."

"Great. Have you heard anything?"

"Not yet, and I don't have any missed calls."

"Ok, talk to you later."

"Bye", he said as he hung up. Emily was the only person he had told that today was the day. His team members at JPL knew he had applied and had been to several meetings, but since the last meeting was more than a month ago, they had mostly forgotten about it.

Mike returned to his office, checked his emails, and returned to his analysis of some recent images.

He heard a knock on his door and looked up to see John, another scientist on the team.

"Are you coming out for lunch?"

"Sure. Sorry, I got lost in that analysis."

"Have you got anything happening this weekend?" asked John as they headed off to the nearest cafeteria.

"It's pretty loose. We might visit Emily's family on Sunday."

"You interested in going to the Dodger's game?"

"Who are they playing?"

"The Reds."

"I'll think about it. Got a bit going on," hedged Mike.

"Ok, but we'll have to get tickets soon."

They entered the cafeteria. Mike ordered a chicken enchilada and John a roast beef sandwich, and they found a table in a not too busy area.

As he took a bite of his enchilada, Mike's phone rang. Jumping up and almost choking, he looked at the number and seeing a 281 prefix definitely increased his adrenalin.

"You right?" asked John.

"I've gotta get this," answered Mike, regaining his breath. "Mike Trellis."

"Hello, Mike. This is Alan Pointer from the NASA Astronaut office in Houston. How's your day going?"

"Ummm, Hi Alan, err, just coughing up an enchilada."

"Great, ahh, glad you are enjoying that. So, it was good to meet you as part of the Astronaut candidate selection process."

"Yes, Alan, it was an interesting and challenging experience." Mike returned John's curious stare as he tried to control his breathing. Fine thing for a potential astronaut to cough their lunch across a room. He could see the cleaner hovering in the background.

"So, Mike. We are impressed by your qualifications, your experience in geoscience, especially at JPL, and the way you participated in the team activities. We would like to offer you a job as an astronaut candidate."

Still standing, he decided sitting was a more dignified option than fainting and managed to say, "Sure".

"I'm certain you'll make a fantastic contribution to our exploration of outer space."

"Thank you, sir. I've wanted this for so long."

"Well, Mike, we will be announcing this in June, so please only tell close family for now. We don't want it leaking before the announcement with the Vice President."

"I understand."

"Okay then, welcome to the team. Someone from our office will be in touch shortly to organise everything."

"Thank you, Alan, I'm honoured, and I look forward to it".

Mike ended the call and put the phone down. He'd just been accepted into one of the most elite groups of people on and off the planet!

"Everything ok?" asked John.

"All my dreams just came true!"

3

Thursday, June 8, 2017

The previous three weeks had been hectic. Mike had immediately rung Emily and told her the good news. Then he had rung his parents, who were thrilled by the news. The following day he'd received a call from a liaison at the astronaut office to organise a trip to Houston to prepare for the announcement, including measurements for his blue uniform. A NASA TV crew had interviewed him. He'd got basic training in handling media questions. He'd had to organise leave from JPL for visits to Houston and give his notice. He never got to that Red's game with John.

Yesterday he'd arrived in Houston with Emily and his folks. He'd meet the other 11 astronaut candidates—a very diverse group, with many women and many were military. Everyone was very excited. They had received their uniform, got more media training and gone through a rehearsal of the announcement.

So now here he was, about to meet the Vice President of the United States of America, and the NASA Administrator and face a press conference!

The other candidates were highly capable. He'd met a couple during the interview process as they gathered in groups of 20, and yesterday they had a chance to get to know each other better. There were only two other scientists, a couple of doctors and several pilots, including a woman, Sue

Bright. Given the current focus on returning to the moon, he wouldn't be surprised if she was part of the first moon mission.

As their names were announced, they entered the auditorium and stood in front of a mock-up of the Orion capsule, internally lit, with the hatch open so the audience could glimpse inside. No longer was this class going to fly in space shuttles and not even, hopefully, the Soyuz. They would train on the Orion, the SpaceX Dragon and the Boeing Starliner. While most of them would no doubt visit the International Space Station (ISS), their focus was on getting to the Moon and Mars.

Mike found Emily and his parents in the crowd and gave them a wave. Not one for large events, still, he took a deep breath and smiled. He figured there would be many more such events in his career, so he'd better get used to them, and he sat on his stool on stage.

The event was a celebration of the candidates and NASA and America's role in space. The NASA Administrator welcomed them to the family. The Vice President of the United States of America, a fan of NASA, commissioned them as future heroes of the country as they ventured back to the Moon and onto Mars, invoking the name of God to bless the class, NASA and the nation. And, of course, there were opportunities for questions from the press.

After the event, many came to shake his hand and congratulate him. Finally, Emily and Mike's parents were able to hug him.

"Mike, we are so proud of you seeing you up there with the rest of the class," said his dad, John.

"Yes, everyone is so skilled and experienced, and fancy 18,000 people applying," his mother Clare said.

"And you got to meet the Vice President!" bubbled Emily.

"I'm not sure a handshake qualifies as 'meeting'," said Mike. "It looks like we are moving on to lunch now, so let's get some food."

They followed the rest of the class into a nearby dining room, finding seats at a table with another astronaut candidate, Christina Pak, and her parents.

"Christina, these are my parents, John and Clare and my girlfriend, Emily," said Mike.

"Mike, thank you," said Christina. "Wonderful to meet you all. These are my parents, Ann and David."

They all greeted each other.

"So, Christina, whereabouts in the States are you from?" asked Clare.

"We live in Orange County, California. My parents moved from South Korea to the US before I was born."

"Oh – such a big city! I don't like big cities. We are from Colorado Springs, and it just keeps growing, but at least it isn't too big. We visited Mike once in LA, but it was just so big and crowded. But I'd guess you all would be used to that."

Mike glared at his mother, changing the subject. "Christina is another of the scientists in the class. You're a biologist, aren't you?"

"Yes, I studied at Berkeley and did my doctorate at Stanford. Currently, I'm working at NASA Ames. Emily, what do you do?"

"Wow, they are great colleges," said Emily. " I'm an intern in robotics on the Mars Rover, Opportunity."

"Okay – so you met Mike at JPL?"

"Yes, we've only been going out a couple of months. This whole astronaut thing has happened so quickly!"

"Doesn't feel like it for me," quipped Mike, "it took two years from when I applied. And that was my second attempt."

"I still can't believe I got through," replied Christina. "Even after all the interviews, I didn't think I had a chance."

The waiter appeared with their set salads, and they settled into a discussion about the application process and their experience of the event. The

NASA Administrator walked around the tables and thanked the families for attending.

At another table, astronaut candidate Sue Bright was eating lunch with her partner, Ron and all of their parents. Alan Pointer, from the Astronaut Office, had joined them.

"Ron, we are thrilled to have a pilot of Sue's calibre as a candidate. I'm afraid we will be taking a lot of her time during the next few years," stated Alan.

"I'm sure. That's not going to be anything new. The Navy has kept her pretty busy."

"That would be true, so I guess you are used to long-distance romance?"

"Well, most of the time I've known her, she has been studying or operating as a test pilot, so she has mostly been at home. Moving to Houston is going to be a big change. I need to try and find some work here."

"Have a chat with our recruitment office. There are few roles that we don't have. I'd be surprised if we couldn't find you something."

"That would be helpful. Thank you, sir."

Ron turned his attention to the turkey sandwich that had just been placed before him.

Sue pondered the discussion. Ron hadn't been overly supportive of the move involved. They'd only just gotten settled into their new place. And he'd only just started a new job as an electrical engineer at a defence contractor, so the idea of moving and a new job just wasn't appealing to him.

4

Sue's parents were surprised by her choice of the Navy for a career. They knew that she'd been interested in space and aviation. After all, she had gone to the Advanced Space Academy during high school. Studying aeronautics at MIT, she was recruited by the US Navy and trained as an F-16 pilot. NASA recruited many good military pilots, so it was a shot to become an astronaut.

Sally Ride's career as a NASA astronaut inspired 12-year-old Sue's imagination. Imagine being in space. Imagine being the first woman to do something. Maybe she could be the first woman on Mars, or perhaps the Moon? She'd figured that flying was the best way to achieve that, and who didn't like planes?

She'd always been more interested in building and doing things than in dolls. She loved hiking and camping, but she'd been obsessed with flying. She also loved watching birds, especially eagles flying. They were so majestic, gliding on the air currents, with barely a movement of a muscle.

Sue's father was an electrical engineer working in power distribution, and her mother was a paediatrician. Their family had always been very focused on science. Her brother worked in software development, and her sister was a paramedic.

Her family had moved fairly frequently when she was a child, as her father moved from project to project. However, they lived in St Louis,

Missouri, for most of her high school years. One of her science teachers was interested in space and often used NASA materials in class, encouraging her to attend the Advanced Space Academy.

Space Academy was fantastic. Sue got to make friends with so many others from around the country who, like her, were interested in science and space. And they got to do simulations of space missions. She even got to be the mission commander!

Sue had been so excited to be accepted to MIT for their aeronautics course. There weren't many women in the class, so she got a lot of interest from the guys. She'd focussed on space systems subjects in her undergrad degree as much as possible. During her final year, a US Navy recruiter had convinced her that she could become a jet pilot, so she signed up.

Training to be a pilot in the US Navy had been tough. While there were now more women in the armed forces, it was still a heavily male-dominated environment. But the guys had been fair and had helped her, and she had been able to help them in return. She was so glad that today it was more usual for a woman to be a fighter pilot. After two deployments, she had completed a Master of Science in Systems Engineering at the Naval Postgraduate School and became a test pilot.

While studying for her masters, Sue met Ron, and in 2015 they had a daughter, Jessica.

The Call had come just after she'd returned from a test flight and was changing out of her flight suit.

"Lieutenant Commander, this is Alan Pointer from the NASA Astronaut office in Houston."

"Good morning, sir."

"Good morning. I hope that you are in a position to talk."

"Yes, sir. All good, sir," she replied as she stood in the changing room in her underwear.

"We at NASA were very impressed by you at the interviews a few weeks ago."

"Thank you, sir."

"Would you still be interested in an astronaut role at NASA?"

"Absolutely, sir!"

"Well, Sue, we would very much like to offer you a position as an Astronaut candidate."

"That is an honour, sir, and I would be excited to accept."

"Great! Well, we will organise for orders to be prepared for you, and you should hear something shortly. Have a great day."

"Thank you, sir. I look forward to the journey. Goodbye."

Sue fist-pumped the sky and then figured she better finish changing before calling Ron.

Suitably attired in her uniform, she called Ron, "Hi Ron, I just heard."

"Did you get it?"

"Yes," she screamed, "I'm going to be an astronaut."

"Wow, ok, then, umm, when do you go?"

"I don't know yet. I'll get orders soon, I guess."

"OK, well, I'm happy for you. We'll talk later. I have to go."

"Right, bye."

Sue looked at the phone. Ron didn't seem all that excited by the prospect. It had been a very long shot, but he knew this was her dream. Ron worked for one of the defense contractors on fighter jets, and he wasn't quite as gung-ho as her fellow pilots. In fact, he was way nerdier, but they'd been able to relate about the engineering systems. And they both loved the outdoors and had several camping adventures under their belt. One of the advantages of not being deployed to a ship!

5

Monday, August 14, 2017

Today was it, the first day of astronaut training. It had been a crazy month for Mike. He'd finished working out his notice at JPL and taken two more trips to Houston while he found a single-bedroom apartment in Clear Lake.

The apartment was pretty nice but basic. One bedroom, walk-in robe, bathroom, small galley kitchen, lounge, dining and a small balcony. The complex had a pool, laundry and gym, and he could have a pet if he wanted. He doubted he would have time, and he'd need to look at buying a house anyway since he expected to be here for years.

Emily was staying in Pasadena as she would be going back to school. Mike suspected their relationship wasn't going to progress.

He'd packed up his apartment in Pasadena, sold a lot of stuff, shipped the rest to Houston, hopped in his RAV4, and began his road trip.

Last week he'd spent a lot of time replacing the stuff he'd sold, such as his couch, bed, dining table and fridge. He had actually camped in his apartment the first night, finding a Chick-fil-A a mile away for dinner. He was now fairly well set up, for a bachelor, and had spent a bit of time familiarising himself with Clear Lake and Houston. How crazy is it when one of the freeways is called 'NASA Bypass' and another main street is 'Space Center Boulevard'!

One thing for sure, it was hot, peaking just under 100 deg F (37 deg C) all week. And humid! Wow. Mike was very glad about the air-conditioning in his car and apartment. And then, there were the cockroaches, flying cockroaches!

So, waking early at 6 am, he jumped out of his new queen size bed, heading out to the pool for a morning swim to stretch out his muscles. He returned home for a shower, dressed in a shirt and tie, and grabbed some cereal.

Mike checked his Facebook. Some Aussie friends seemed to be laughing at their deputy Prime Minister turning out to be a New Zealander. What a laugh. Less of a laugh was the news of the landslides in Freetown, Sierra Leone, killing 500. That put things in a bit of perspective.

Taking a selfie and recalling the need to manage his public profile, he posted, "First day training as an astronaut!"

He grabbed his things and headed to his RAV4 to drive to the Johnson Space Center (JSC).

JSC was the home of the NASA Astronaut Corps, with most based here and much of the training located here or nearby.

After navigating through security, Mike found his way to the correct car park and into the NASA Astronaut Office, where he found several other candidates already gathered.

Alan Pointer walked over to Mike, extending his hand. "Mike, good to see you. Have you got settled in?"

"Yes, thanks, Alan. I've got an apartment in Clear Lake while I have a look around for somewhere to buy."

"Good idea. There are a lot of places available, and you'll be around here for several years, so a good time to buy. Did your move go ok?"

"Yes, got everything packed up. The drive was fun, and my stuff arrived last week."

"Great! We will get started in about 20 minutes, so grab yourself a coffee or juice. There're some donuts over there. Don't expect them every day, but we wanted you folks to feel welcome and help you settle in."

"Ok, thanks, Alan."

Mike looked around the room, heading straight to the coffee.

"Hi Mike, welcome to Houston."

Mike turned to see who it was. He said, "Christina, good to see you. How did your move go?"

"Pretty busy. While we were here in June, I looked at a few houses with realtors and purchased one, moving in just last week. I'm still living in boxes!"

"Wow, organised! I'm renting an apartment. I'm going to look around and see what I like. Real estate is much cheaper here than near JPL, so I guess buying makes sense.

"So, what do you think today holds?"

"I suspect a lot of briefings and hand-holding!"

"Hi, Christina, Mike. You going to let someone else get at the donuts?"

Mike turned to see Sue, smartly dressed in a pantsuit.

"Sure, Sue, I guess we better get something."

They poured themselves coffees, Christina got an orange juice, and Mike selected a doughnut. Another candidate, Andrew Glover, joined them.

"Damn hot and humid here," said Andrew.

"Yes", agreed Mike and Christina.

"Gets this bad in Maryland in summer," commented Sue.

"I prefer desert," said Andrew. "You guys got any idea who should be class leaders?"

"I reckon Sue here would be a good leader," offered Mike.

"I agree," said Christina.

Sue was blushing now. "I think it's a bit early to know who the top dogs are quite yet."

Just then, they heard Alan calling the group to attention.

"Folks. Welcome again to Johnson Space Centre. If you want to make your way into the briefing room, we will get underway shortly."

The group made their way into the room, finding seats. They didn't need to wait long.

"Good Morning. Welcome to Johnson Space Center. My name is Chris Forest, and I'm NASA's Chief Astronaut.

"Ladies and gentlemen, you have begun a journey of exploration. Yes, of space, the Moon and even Mars, but also of yourselves. You have been chosen from amongst the largest group of applicants in NASA history. You already excel in diverse careers, of which you can be rightly proud.

"From today, you are no longer leaders. You are rookies. You will discover that you have so much more to learn, and we will help you with that. You will have to learn to become a team, trust each other, work together and save each other's lives when there is no one else to help.

"You are going to need to learn how to cope when you are isolated in a tin can with three of your crew with only a comms channel to link you with home. You will have to learn systems, learn science, and learn to live without gravity.

"This class is 'doing the next thing'. We expect you will not just go into earth orbit but go and live on the Moon and Mars. You will fly in spacecraft that have not yet been designed! And, to do that, you are going to have to cope with situations that we have only yet dreamed about, and you will have to solve them.

"We will help you. We will train you. We will test you. We will invest in you. We will annoy you! And you will deal with it, and you will ask for help because failure is not possible. And you will fail if you don't ask for help. And then, once again, you'll be leaders.

"Mental health is one of the biggest factors we in the Astronaut Corps deal with. You will have problems, and it is Okay to ask for help. You all have just moved, some with families, and you have just changed jobs. For anybody, that is a stressful situation. If you are struggling, start asking for help now. NASA needs you healthy in all aspects.

"Being in space is fantastic. It is like nothing else, and I hope and expect that all of you will one day experience that. I suspect some of you will experience things I haven't, such as walking on the Moon or Mars. Do take the time to experience those things. Remember them, record them. That is what will make the work and the discomfort, and the frustrations, worthwhile.

"Class of 2017, welcome to NASA."

Everyone applauded.

Alan took the floor as Chris Forest sat down.

"Thank you, Chris. Candidates, the next two years are going to be very busy. You are going to visit all of NASA. You need to know what we do because one of your roles is Public Relations, and another is staff morale. You will encourage and motivate the staff by turning up at a facility. That will take some getting used to. You will also need to learn Russian, the basics of the ISS systems and the spacecraft you will fly, including the Soyuz, Orion, and other vehicles, and train in EVA operations. All before you are approved as Astronauts and be available for selection for a mission. And then you'll do more learning. You will be learning for the rest of your career.

"So, today, you will meet the team and get an orientation to JSC.

"Also, as a group, you need to select your class leaders over the next week. Be ready next week to tell me who they are."

Then the briefing began.

6

Tuesday, April 12 2018

Sue struggled into the extravehicular mobility unit (aka EVA suit) with the help of the suit technicians. It was not easy. On earth, the suit was actually very heavy. This was the first time that she was going into the Neutral Buoyancy Laboratory (NBL) for training. Mike was her training partner. It made sense to have a pilot train with a mission specialist.

The last nine months had been as busy as promised. Most weeks, the class visited one facility or another. There had been survival training., and they'd had a geology field trip. She'd even got to learn and perform maintenance on the T-38 jets. But this exercise was probably the closest to being in space that she'd come. The ISS trainer mock-up was close, but you weren't floating. In the NBL, she'd be floating as she would in space, in a space suit!

Her partner Ron had settled in ok. They'd bought a red brick 3,500 square foot, two-storey 4 bedroom house in Seabrook. Ron had managed to find some remote work so he could stay home and look after their now three-year-old daughter, Jessica. He still didn't seem to be overly happy, but he was supportive. Being a young mother and Astronaut Candidate was a tricky combination. However, NASA understood, with many candidates also having young families. Jessica was now old enough for them to let her be in childcare a few days a week, and Ron could focus more on work.

Sue was finally properly in the legs and bottom half of the suit, and it was time to climb into the torso. The assistants helped her get under the torso and climb up into it. There wasn't a lot of room to move, and the lower part of the suit weighed her down. After several minutes of struggle, she finally got her arms into the sleeves and her head out the neck and rested while the team secured the lower half of the suit to the torso. Then they fit her gloves and added the weights to make her neutrally buoyant in the tank.

Sue could just make out Mike going through the same process nearby. The process took over an hour, and most of it had to be performed with others' assistance. She imagined what this task would be like for just two people on the moon helping each other. The suits wouldn't have the same weight there, but it would still be awkward and even slower.

Mike seemed a sensible guy to her. He was driven in different ways from the military guys she had spent most of her Navy life with. In some ways, not unlike Ron. More thoughtful, and, well, somewhat geekish, and definitely fitter. They got on fairly well, but this was the first time they'd been on the same team. That was probably part of the training, she thought. She had noticed that teams were mixed up, and they were constantly being monitored by trainers, especially on the various training trips they had undertaken, such as the survival and geology training trips.

Finally, they were both ready and standing on the platform, back to back, prepared to be lifted into the pool. Given the all-clear, the pneumatic crane lifted them up, across and then down into the pool, where final leak checks were performed and tweaks made to the weights on the suits to ensure they were neutrally buoyant. The pressure in the suits was above atmospheric pressure to counter the water pressure. The suit air mix had less nitrogen and a greater oxygen concentration. The training was expected to last about 6 hours, so measures were required to avoid the bends.

As the water washed over her helmet, Sue controlled her breathing. She had done Scuba training, so she was familiar with being underwater, but this was different. The air blowing into the suit was somewhat noisy, and if something went wrong, it wasn't as simple as swimming to the surface and taking a face mask off. In fact, the briefings and training had been very clear on procedures to clear their ears. A former astronaut, Leland Melvin, had been injured during such training when the Valsalva device used for this purpose was missing.

"Control to EV1. Are you ready to proceed?" she heard through her headset.

"EV1 Roger," Sue replied.

"Control to EV2. Are you ready to proceed?"

"EV2, copy that. Ready to proceed," Mike sounded nervous.

"Control to divers take EV1 and 2 down to 10 feet."

Sue felt them move down. Wearing the suit, there was no way that she could propel herself, so divers moved her around. She felt the pressure build in her ears and used the Valsalva device to clear her ears. She tried forming fists with her hands. There was resistance, but she could do it. Looking around, she was amazed at how clear the water was.

"EV2 to Control, I'm having trouble clearing my ears."

Also by David Miller

Artemis 3

First published 2023 by David Miller in Australia

Published by Firmament Books.

ISBN 978-0-6457134-0-4 (E-book) 978-0-6457134-1-1 (Paperback) 978-0-6457134-2-8 (Hardback)

Cover Design: Book Cover Design by 100 Covers. Original cover created by Tim Young from public images, including the NASA images archive.

firmamentbooks.com

davidmiller.online

Afterword

I finished this short book when Artemis II rolled out to the launch pad, and when people commemorated the Challenger accident's 40th anniversary. Exploring space is not without risk, but NASA have learnt, sometimes the hard way, how to manage that risk.

It turns out that the first fast transfer to the ISS by a SOYUZ was in 2018. There was an incident in the past where there was a water leak in an astronaut's helmet during a spacewalk. You can watch on YouTube! Space suits do need to get replaced and mission plans change. And, there really is a Canadian flying on Artemis II.

If you want to read what I think could happen on Artemis 3 and see what happens with George, please read my book Artemis 3!

www.ingramcontent.com/pod-product-compliance
Lightning Source LLC
LaVergne TN
LVHW010626100826
845148LV00014B/3123